The
Western

Home

Stories for Home on the Range

Catherine Cooper

PEDLAR PRESS | ST JOHN'S

ACKNOWLEDGEMENTS
The publisher wishes to thank the Canada Council for the Arts and the NL Publishers Assistance Program for their generous support of our publishing program.

LIBRARY AND ARCHIVES CANADA
CATALOGUING IN PUBLICATION

Cooper, Catherine, 1982-, author
   The western home / Catherine Cooper.

Short stories.
ISBN 978-1-897141-60-1 (pbk.)

   1. Home on the range (Song)--Fiction. I. Title.

PS8605.O654W48 2014   C813'.6   C2013-907865-7

COVER ART Anandraj Thiyagarajaperumal, *Big Mammoth in Yellowstone Park*, 2013

DESIGN Zab Design & Typography, Toronto

TYPEFACE Galliard, Carter & Cone Typefoundry

Printed in Canada

for Paul, who gave my life its bent

Contents

Stories

From "No Place" to Home: The Quest for a Western
Home in Brewster Higley's "Home on the Range"

The We

stern Home

This is the original home
at the heart of brutalist design.
No storm can slam its shape apart.
No thief can carry it off like a tent.
It dwells in ashen buildings where
  the present sleeps.

—FANNY HOWE

1872
The Western Home

IN THE MORNING, Brewster sat under the apple tree by the creek, sipping whisky mixed with grainy coffee dregs. Honey, his horse, was next to him, eating grass and swishing her tail at flies. It was getting hot, and soon he would be forced indoors for the rest of the day. He was trying to enjoy the scenery, but he felt anxious and didn't want to be alone with his thoughts. He didn't want company, either; most people who came brought bad news, and the more time he spent alone the harder it was to seem normal in conversation. "No hope for us, Honey," he said when she started to nuzzle around his hair and beard. He held his half-empty bottle up to the light and told himself that soon it wouldn't matter what news came, since there was nothing he could do for anyone if he couldn't stay on his horse.

He tried to forget his anxious thoughts and focus on the creek, which was so comforting when he was in the right frame of mind. To his left, the grass gave way to coarse sand where the water gathered in a small pool under a cottonwood.

On the opposite bank was a patch of motley briars. Beyond that, there was the tree line, which separated Brewster from a view that he liked, but not first thing in the morning when he emerged sick and lonely from his dugout.

When he left Indiana, he had worn the imprints of Mercy's incisors on his left shoulder.

"You've ruined me!" he had screamed, and he had thrown his boiled potato at her head, but hit the wall instead. The flaky, overcooked potato created a surprisingly dramatic explosion on impact.

He was almost insane with rage, but in his other mind, which had watched the scene with detached curiosity, he knew he would have to leave. Whenever he made a mistake or things got too bad to bear, he reminded himself that eventually he would be going. He had to be quite sure that he had finished making mistakes first, however, because once he had found a place to settle down, he didn't plan to move again.

He rinsed his cup in the creek and walked back to the dugout, struggling to pull open the door. He still wasn't used to the structure, which gave the impression of having been partially reclaimed by the hillock into which it was built. He took two steps down into the darkness, leaving his cup on the ground next to the door, not bothering, as he had done in the beginning, to take off his shoes. Inside, the air was mouldy and damp, the floor and walls giving off a moist, cool smell.

"Damn," he said when he sifted through his flour and found weevils. "Damn you," he said to them, narrowing his eyes. He shoved the sack to the back of the shelf and took down a can of beans, then made two toddling steps to the other side of the room and sat in the chair. He opened the can with his knife, forming four sharp metal peaks.

Looking up through the doorway he saw only dim shapes against the white sky. The tree was a formless green shadow. Hazy bodies moved in the leaves and took off. Brewster recited some verses to himself as he watched this undefined world outside. Sometimes it happened this way. He would walk around with a line in his mind for a week or more before writing it down, and in many cases that was how he sorted the great lines from those that would have ended up in the fire had he recorded them. Paper was scarce, and he was so sensitive to his own bad poetry that even once it was burned it continued to haunt him and often kept him from writing the next time.

Almost all of his poetry had been disappointing. Once he had written something sentimental about his mother, but it was really a fantasy since he couldn't remember her. Another time, he had written some painfully precious verses dedicated to Dryden, which had only been saved from the fire by being favoured—whether sincerely or not, he couldn't tell—by Catherine. His best, he felt, was "Army Blue," written after Catherine died, at the end of the war, before he met Mercy. He was hurt that his children didn't care about that poem. He had expected Stella, at least, to say that she liked it and ask him to read it again. And he would for once have been happy to see a tear in Arthur's eyes, which remained dry even after his father's rousing delivery of the final lines: "*Now, fellows, we must say goodbye. We've stuck our four years through. Our future is a cloudless sky. We'll don the Army Blue.*"

Arthur's face had been deformed with crying when he was forced to let go of Brewster's sleeve at the train station, and it had worried Brewster that the boy was still so effeminate at the age of ten. If Brewster looked at him with any hint of rebuke, Arthur's lip would begin to quiver. Once Brewster slapped his hand when he caught him stealing a piece of cake, and afterward Arthur didn't speak for a week. Stella, on the other hand, was like her father. Twelve years old, motherless, but all she said was a flat, "Goodbye, father," before turning to board the train. She had not asked the real reason why she and Arthur were being sent away. That she wasn't going to be left with Mercy was good enough.

Mercy was terrible with his children, as she was terrible in general. She brushed Stella's hair as if she were whipping a horse, and she didn't care how much Stella complained or how much hair came out in the process. Arthur she ignored unless he cried, and then she would smack him, which made him hysterical. Everything she did and everything she said and even everything she cooked was cruel, and that was what had originally attracted Brewster to her. He thought he wanted that at first—her austerity, her mean way of doing things, always using each scrap of material, rubbing the last drop out of every tin with a heel of bread, boiling things until they were unrecognizable and serving them without salt. But soon he became like a mulish adolescent. He hated her, and it was all her fault. If he drank it was her fault, and if people went to the next county to see a doctor it was her fault and if his children were growing up miserable and strange it was also her fault.

When he left Indiana, he did not say goodbye to her at all. The potato fight had been their final communication.

The following week, while she was away visiting her mother, he put Stella and Arthur on a train to Illinois, borrowed a revolver from a neighbour, and simply cleared out. He left no forwarding address and no further clues as to where any of them had gone, only the keys in the hiding place and his wedding ring on the kitchen table—enough to make sure she understood that their disappearance was deliberate, planned and permanent. In his more generous moments, he told himself that she would be happy to have peace without them.

He heard someone coming and jumped to his feet so quickly he had to grab the table to steady himself, tipping over the can of beans. He flattened his shirt with the palms of his hands and felt for traces of food in his beard.

"You're needed, Dr. Higley," someone shouted. Brewster emerged to see Dan Hibberd looking sweaty and agitated. His horse was frothing at the mouth, which Brewster knew was a bad sign, Hibberd not being the type of man to push his animals so hard. He held his hand in a kind of salute to shield his eyes from the sun.

"By whom?" he said.

"We were making a clearing and a tree fell on Coates's leg. It took four of us pulling like all wrath to get him out of there."

"Where is he?"

"Munro's."

Brewster went inside and came back as quickly as he could with his kit and hat tucked under his arm. He saddled Honey in silence while Hibberd led his horse to drink at the creek. When he was ready, Brewster took his handsaw from where it hung by the door and tied it to Honey's saddle.

The heat was overwhelming and Brewster felt sick, so he was grateful to Hibberd for not trying to make conversation. He was in no state to keep up a canter, either, as he could tell Hibberd was anxious to do. Sweat ran down his back and through his wiry black beard as he tried to prepare himself by thinking over possible scenarios for blunt force injuries.

He had trained in otolaryngology, but in Kansas he had to be ready for anything. Sometimes the work disgusted him, had especially when he was younger. He hadn't wanted to be a physician then, and even now he didn't. He had only wanted to find a way to be indispensable. But now that he was almost fifty, and his best years of work were behind him, he had learned to like certain aspects of the job. It was the only time in his life when he was able to focus completely on the present, and time passed differently. When he was drunk, time passed differently too, but there was always that sober self in the back of his consciousness who was filled with self-loathing, and he couldn't drink enough to quiet it without passing out.

When they arrived at the Munro place, Coates was lying on the kitchen table, and three men—Munro, Chesley and Barnes—sat silently in chairs set around the room. Mrs. Munro stood at the head of the table holding a damp cloth to Coates's forehead.

Brewster had only ever met Munro's wife incidentally, he had never spoken to her, and he wished that she weren't there. Coates Brewster knew as an irritating and energetic kid who was always trying to prove himself by doing more than he was able or by making up lies about what he had done. His mother was Swedish, so from time to time he had translated when Brewster was treating a Swede who spoke no English.

Brewster could sense that the men felt awkward, as people often do after accidents, when they can still hear the echo of some shrill scream they uttered in the initial moment of panic. When Brewster and Dan walked in, all three jumped up.

"Hello Ma'am," Brewster said to Mrs. Munro. He gave a slight bow before moving toward his patient, whose leg had been bound in a makeshift splint. "Hello George," he said. He leaned on the table and wiped the sweat from his forehead and neck with the back of his sleeve. "What happened?"

"A tree fell on my leg," Coates said. He pointed at the limb dismissively. "We were clearing the pasture." He was calm and pallid, in shock.

Brewster asked Coates to relax while he cut his trousers away. Once the limb was bare, it was as Brewster had predicted. The skin was not broken, but the shin was severely bruised, and a quick examination told him that below the knee the leg was bloodless and dead.

He took out a piece of dry cloth from his kit and passed it to Mrs. Munro. "Hold this loosely over his mouth and nose," he said.

"Munro," he said, turning to her husband. "Find some strong thread, and boil it." Brewster took the bottle of ether from his kit and dripped it on the cloth that Mrs. Munro was holding over Coates's mouth. "Don't breathe it in yourself," he said, passing her the bottle.

He went to the trough outside to splash cold water on his face. When he returned, he poured alcohol on Coates's leg and on his scalpel. Without breaking the skin he made his mark with the tip of the blade, leaving as a guide a semi-lunar scratch ending above the knee. Coates didn't move or make a sound.

"What are you going to do?" asked Mrs. Munro.

"Turn your face away from that," he said.

"You can't…" she said.

He looked up at her with the intention of saying something reassuring, but he was surprised by the antagonism in her expression. He turned away. "Chesley, come and hold up his leg so I can mark the underside," he said.

"Couldn't we give it a day or two?" Mrs. Munro said as Brewster completed his marks on the other side of Coates's leg. "It's only bruised."

"I'm sorry," he said, and then Coates began to heave. It took both Chesley and Barnes to help him turn Coates onto his side so that gravity could do its work. Once Coates's mouth had been cleared and his breathing was thick and raspy, Brewster made the first incision, cutting through the skin and fat like cold butter, separating the tough white sheath of fascia to reveal the russet quadriceps muscle. When he cut through the nerve, the knee contracted and Chesley shouted because he thought Coates was awake. "It's involuntary," Brewster said, without looking up.

When he had finished cutting the muscle on the front of the leg, he used his index finger to hook the femoral artery, vein and nerve all at once. "String," he said. Munro gave him the right amount without being told. He tied a double knot both above and below his incision then cut the veins and nerve all at once. "Lift it again," he said. Chesley took up the leg and held it firmly at a forty-five-degree angle above the mess on the table.

Brewster sliced through skin and tendons, breaking them from each side and working toward the middle. He asked for string again and hooked, tied off and severed the popliteal. Now Coates's femur was exposed above his knee. "Hibberd, get my saw," Brewster said. Dan, who remembered that it was tied to Honey's saddle, went outside. While he waited, Brewster felt hungry. His bladder was full. His arms were weak. He wanted a drink.

He had done plenty of surgeries in much worse states. He could be as drunk or sick or depressed as anything, but as soon as he had to work, his mind became sharp. Once the saw was disinfected, he forgot his body again. He worked his way through Coates's bone, blowing the white bone dust away to keep his field clear, and Chesley coughed as it entered his nose and mouth but continued to hold Coates's leg steady.

When Brewster was through the bone, the amputated portion of the leg fell into Chesley's hands. Chesley placed it gently at the end of the table then ran outside, letting the door slam behind him. "I'll need the rest of that thread," Brewster said to Munro, "and a strong needle." He noticed Mrs. Munro looking at his shaking hands, so he held them flat on the table. She left the cloth resting on Coates's face while she found and threaded a needle herself. In silence, Brewster stitched the fascia and muscle over the severed bone and sewed the flaps of skin neatly together.

"You can take the cloth off his face now," he said when he had finished. He gestured to Munro to come and help him turn George on his side. "Hold his jaw forward," he said to Mrs. Munro, and he caught her eye for the first time since she had shot him that look, but he couldn't read her expression.

He told the men how to care for Coates and instructed them to burn the leg.

"God, I think I puked up everything I've et since I left Tennessee," Chesley said as Brewster passed him on his way outside to wash his hands, followed by Munro.

"Why don't you stay?" Munro asked. "I'll have Mrs. Munro make you something to eat."

"No," Brewster said. "That's kind of you, but I won't stay." He dried his hands on his shirt and then paused, inspecting his fingernails.

"Listen, Doc," Munro said. "We got no money to give you right now, but I'll send someone of George's up to pay you." Brewster believed that the men had nothing to give him if they said so, and he was sure that he would be paid eventually. He wanted to leave quickly, though, hoping to spare himself the humiliation of asking Munro to give him some whisky in the meantime.

"Oh, I almost forgot," Munro said, leaning in. "There's a man arrived from Indiana yesterday. He says he wants to see you. You're from Indiana, right?"

Brewster didn't answer.

"What part of Indiana?"

"I'm really from Ohio," Brewster said. "I don't want to ride home in the dark."

"It's not dark for a long time yet," Munro said, but Brewster, who had already mounted his horse, pretended not to hear.

As soon as he was out of sight of Munro's place he stopped and turned sidesaddle to have a piss without dismounting. Once his bladder was empty, he became aware of his other worries.

It was unlikely that he would know this man from Indiana, but the way Munro had said "he wants to see you"—Still, even if the man did know him, what difference did it make? It was more embarrassing than anything. He didn't want people to look at him with pity any more than he wanted them to look at him with suspicion. He really didn't want them to look at him at all. He tried to comfort himself with the thought that if things went sour he could leave Smith County. It wasn't the first time it had occurred to him. It was a familiar feeling, the urge to move on. But when he encountered men like Hibberd and Barnes and Trube Reese, he was sorry that it was so, which was more than he could say for any other place he had lived.

In Kansas, people were generally kind, occasionally he could socialize and feel fine with them, and they never called on him unless it was an emergency. In Indiana, people would send their children around to his house, sometimes in the middle of the night. The children couldn't be relied on to give accurate descriptions of the patients' complaints, so every time Brewster had to go or risk being blamed for someone's death, but in most cases it was something that had to be waited out. In Kansas, patients were brought to him whenever possible, and when he was asked to come, he never felt taken for granted, and no one ever questioned his judgement. He was quite sure, for instance, that even if Coates had been in his right mind, he wouldn't have questioned the decision to amputate his leg. It would be hard to find such a young man in Indiana, Brewster thought.

As he rode home in the eerie quiet of early evening, he thought about his own children. He had three living, one of whom, his namesake, he wouldn't recognize if they passed each other in the street. Besides them, there were another two who had died as infants. The first of these was born to his first wife, Marie, who died herself a year after the baby. He couldn't remember that baby's face at all. It had looked like every other dead baby he had seen. The second, Catherine's, was too horrific to think of.

In general, Brewster found it too painful to think about Catherine, but there was nothing he could do to stop it once he began, so he chose one memory of her to keep coming back to. When she was alive they had lived in a tiny house they'd chosen because of its location on the banks of a river. He had always liked burning things, ever since he was a child, and burning the grass on the banks after the thaw was his favourite rite of spring. He liked to stand on top of the hill and watch the fire, secretly wishing that it would get out of control and burn down the house and the neighbour's houses too. Catherine never asked him not to, but he knew she hated it: if the wind was blowing in the wrong direction she could never get the smell of smoke out of the curtains.

One day when he was setting one of his fires, he looked back at the house and saw Catherine closing a window. The look on her face was such a miraculous combination of love and resignation, he never forgot it. Catherine shaped herself around his life like a tree that grows where it can. And although it took some time for him to understand why that moment had stayed with him and come to represent the whole life of the only person he had ever truly loved, he eventually saw that he had always wished for that kind of simplicity of spirit, which seemed to come so naturally to her and which he could never cultivate no matter how hard he tried.

He came out past the trees to get a better view of the Solomon River Valley now lit by the sunset. There were no animals in sight apart from a small group of sharptail grouse looking for grasshoppers, unaware of his presence. He ran his fingers through Honey's mane and told her she was a good girl as he watched the birds pecking all around them.

He had always had rural dreams, but the particular idea of Kansas seemed to have come from nowhere. Once, not long after he married Mercy, he'd seen a painting that involved an image of huge buttes and a deep river valley with a tiny human figure so far in the distance you had to look closely to decipher the black spot on the landscape. In fact it was an advertisement, and that was its trick—to make you look more closely. Brewster had been struck by the effect and had stared at the painting for ages. He wanted to be like that lone figure, placed there only to provide a sense of scale. He thought that the daily reminder of his own insignificance would put things in perspective and make him feel his place.

But when he finally arrived in Kansas, he didn't feel much of anything. It was mid-winter, and when he rode into Gaylord with his travelling companions his hands and feet were numb. He hadn't been willing to accept it when the other men told him that even if he did claim his land, there was no way to build a dugout before the thaw. Finally, his inquiries all inspiring unconcealed chuckles from the locals, he had no choice but to resign himself to the impossibility of his original plan and rent a room at Matt Gilman's boarding house.

This arrangement was torture. It wasn't that he wanted to be alone—he was almost unbearably lonely, and he knew that if he could make people trust him, they wouldn't mind the rest—but when he drank he often had lapses of memory and would wake up in a state of terror, wondering what he had done. He was afraid that despite his best efforts he was becoming ridiculous to the other settlers, like a character in a pantomime. Once he had woken with a crust of bread clutched in his hand, and it wasn't until days later that he remembered watching a woman through a window as she took bread out of her oven, him outside in the cold wanting it so badly, not only the bread, but the woman and the home as well.

When the snow began to melt, he hired a locator who found him his land on the first day. The creek and the trees made it a practical place to settle, and it was beautiful, as he had imagined. The following morning, he left for the United States Land Office in Concordia and paid fourteen dollars and fifty cents for his deed. Then he and Trube Reese, who had needed his gallbladder out in a hurry but had no capital, had built the dugout, where Brewster could live quite comfortably until he could afford to build a proper log cabin.

It was ideal, in a way, but it had never lived up to his expectations. He hadn't anticipated all the gossip and petty politics, and he had yet to see a buffalo—instead, when spring came, all he saw were flies and sunflowers. He had never seen so many flowers of any kind in one place. Scores of flowers. He had thought about Stella, remembered a silly song she had made up, being preoccupied with death, as lonely children often are. "Everything lives to die," she sang in a monotone, "a flower blooms to die." Catherine had found it funny and encouraged her to sing it. But when Catherine herself was dying, Stella wouldn't be in the same room as her. Brewster still couldn't understand how his daughter could have stayed away when he himself had spent so much of his life wishing he'd had a chance to know his mother. "She smells," Stella said once when he asked her why she didn't keep her mother company, and he slapped her for that.

Catherine's death was the worst thing in his life, and he would have given almost anything to forget it, but he always ended up back there. He had left the birth to a midwife—his first mistake—and settled himself in behind the bar at a local hotel. By the time Arthur came to tell him what was happening, it was too late. When he walked into the room, the baby's limp, purple body hung hideously between Catherine's legs, its head trapped inside her.

"Why the hell didn't you send someone sooner?" he shouted at the midwife, who continued her useless attempt to clean up the blood. He took the scissors from his doctor's kit, which he kept by the front door, and Catherine screamed as he pressed them into the nape of the baby's neck. He stirred around to break up the brain matter, and white fluid leaked out, decompressing the skull. Though he tried his best to soothe her, Catherine would not stay still, and her writhing made it impossible for him to be sure he wasn't damaging her with the scissors. Once the head had been released, the midwife wrapped the small body in a receiving blanket and took it away.

It quickly became clear that something had gone terribly wrong. Catherine was leaking urine and pus, and the smell in the room was terrible. He was afraid to examine her, because he didn't want to know what he had done. In the end it made no difference. She could not have survived the tiny hole the scissors had made in her bladder.

He took care of her for three months. When the pain became too bad he gave her morphine. He got used to the smell. He read stories aloud to her in bed. He cleaned her and tried to be cheerful. He cooked awful meals. He borrowed money from the last people in town who would lend to him: he accepted the shame of taking money from her family.

After she died, the rumours began, supported by the fact that he had neither paid for nor attended the funeral. He'd dressed himself that morning in his only decent suit, but he couldn't convince himself to walk out the door. Catherine's brother began to tell people that she would have survived if she had received proper medical treatment. He went around town announcing that Brewster was a drunk and a neglectful husband and a criminally negligent physician, that he had caused the injury that killed Catherine and had done nothing to treat it. The midwife was no doubt at it too, and as the rumours spread people began to say that his first wife had died mysteriously as well.

So he'd been destitute, an outcast, twice a widower and once divorced, a drunk and a father of two—three if you counted his namesake, who lived with his grandparents in Ohio. Under those circumstances, Mercy—a spinster who would have been willing to marry almost anyone to escape her own mother—was the only woman who would have him. She would cook and clean and take care of his children, and living with her personality seemed fitting to him. Happiness would have been impossible, and if it had been possible, it would have been unthinkable. But Mercy wasn't entirely bad. She had her moments. Sometimes she sang when she was working, and she made wonderful pies. He imagined her finding pieces of that exploded potato months later, cleaning them from hidden places in that dark kitchen in Indiana, which was now hers alone.

He let Honey drink at the river for a while and then continued toward his dugout. It had begun to rain gently, and he was anxious to get back to his whisky, his blanket and his beans. Maybe he would write down some verses. It occurred to him that he might have left the door open in his haste to leave, and coyotes might have been attracted by the smell of food and taken over the place. He gave Honey a gentle kick. He wanted to be home before dark.

1956
Sugar Arts

EUGENE INHERITED his love of sweets from his mother, who was fat and indulgent and hated America from the day she arrived to the day she died. She did her best to make the family's farm in Aroostook a little England, with lots of rich puddings that ruined her son's palate as well as his capacity for moderation. Now, as an adult, he is famous for his devotion to sweets, which he enjoys without much discernment, except that he generally finds things taste better if they are English.

His shop, Sugar Arts, has a sherbet-green stucco facade. In one of the display windows there are fourteen cardboard cakes. A stack of patterned hatbox confections topped with a pink lady's hat. A pile of pastel lettered blocks finished with a blue rattle and trimmed with golden bells. A classic three-tier with red garland icing and a silver horseshoe ring around a plastic bride and groom. In the other window are pastries and sweets, all carefully arranged. Inside, the warm smile Eugene wears while serving a customer evaporates as he enters the kitchen, where a girl with stretch-marked arms and rotten teeth carefully turns out delicate pink sugar roses for the Watson-Easton wedding cake.

Eugene is a thin man with a rough face, lines drawing deep parentheses around his mouth. Today, as usual, he is wearing long sleeves rolled up to his elbows and a fresh white cotton apron. People generally assume that he is well liked, since he always seems to be happy. To his face they call him "The Late Mr. Ingamels," because he is never on time. Behind his back they say he is not serious, that he owes everything to his sensible wife.

This morning, Eugene put a bag of pink marshmallow fish into the hand of his youngest daughter, who was named after his beloved aunt in England. "These are only for you, Evie," he said as he pressed her fingers closed around the sweets. "Say thank you, Daddy," he said. The fish bulged at the head and tail as Evelyn squeezed them in her palm, but their spongy bodies regained their shapes when she released them into the pocket of her navy school pinafore.

It is rare for Eugene to give even Evelyn something so whole and perfect. Failed sugar flowers, collapsed cakes, discoloured butter cream icing and misshapen fondant figurines are stowed in his lunch box and distributed daily to all of his children behind their mother's back. But perfect pink fish brought from the shop in a bag and tied with a silver ribbon is something so rare as to be almost a burden to Evelyn, and it isn't long before she wishes he hadn't given them to her at all.

At school, she puts her hand into her pocket again and

again to make sure that they are still there, and each time she reminds herself to hide them as soon as she gets home, so that her mother won't see.

Chris talks to herself as she waters her tomatoes, repeating everything that needs to be done. She will have to cut back the raspberry bushes soon. "If only he would do that sort of thing," she says. Her hands are rough and sun-spotted, and her finger is bleeding where a thorn has cut it.

Chris is both wife and mother to Eugene, but she offers only the functions of these roles and none of their comforts. She is a careful and practical woman, impatient with her husband's financial failings and his fantasies about moving the family back to England. She feeds her children as well as her resources allow, never guessing that they are being raised on sugar. She tries to fill them with substantial things, like the lettuce that she has just picked for their supper, but to varying degrees they have all been ruined by their father, especially Evelyn.

In the evening, when Eugene comes home from work, he has confectioners' sugar in his hair and on his clothes, and Chris sends him to the shower. She doesn't lose her temper when he is late to the table, and she doesn't panic when she finds him lying on the bathroom floor. She makes the children stay at the table until the ambulance arrives, so Evelyn sees only a quick glimpse of her father's body on the stretcher. His eyes are open, and his wet hair has soaked the pillow beneath it, leaving a dark halo around his head.

One day shortly after Eugene's collapse in the bathroom, Chris sends Evelyn to deliver handkerchiefs to him at the hospital on her way to school. Chris will not visit him herself. She has been furious with him since learning that he allowed people from the congregational church to perform a faith healing service on his behalf. She says that he is breaking up the family, and she makes Evelyn promise not to talk to "those people" if they are there.

Evelyn keeps the handkerchiefs in her school bag, pressed between two books so they won't wrinkle. When Eugene sees them he looks like he might cry. He has saved her the pudding that came with his supper the night before, a plastic cup with a piece of date cake in it. A nurse comes to say that a family friend is waiting to visit.

"Go to school," Eugene says. When she leans in to kiss him goodbye, he catches her wrist and whispers in her ear, "Come and see me on your way home. I have something important to tell you."

That day Martha Stein invites Evelyn to her house after school, and because Martha is rich and popular, Evelyn goes. In the evening, Chris receives a phone call from Eugene's doctor, who says that Eugene has taken a turn for the worse and the children shouldn't visit unless his condition improves. "We don't want them to remember him like this," he says. Evelyn tries to explain to Chris that her father has something important to tell her, but Chris says that rules are rules and it will have to wait.

On the evening of the day Eugene dies, Chris sits all four of her children around the table. The others start to bawl right away, and Chris puts her arms around them, but Evelyn stares at them as if they were strangers. She doesn't believe what her mother has said. It's the Friday before the summer holidays, and her only thought is that she won't get any extra time off school since it's the holidays anyway.

At the funeral, she can't believe how small the coffin is, and she knows she is right not to believe what everyone is saying about her father being dead, because he couldn't possibly fit into such a small box. After the ceremony, the people gather outside the church. Someone puts his hand on Evelyn's head and tells Chris, "She's the one you're going to have to look out for."

"She was the only one he ever bothered with," Chris says.

That night Evelyn dreams that she rides her bike to the graveyard. She carries a spade on the back. At her father's grave she digs up the coffin and opens it, and her father is in there, alive. He says *I knew you'd be the only one who wouldn't believe I was dead*. They walk together to the house, stopping by the raspberry bushes at the back gate. White moonlight shines in his thin, pale hair, and he reaches out to her like a lover in a movie.

When she wakes up from the dream, the same white moon is burning through her window. She remembers her dream and jumps out of bed, utterly convinced that he is alive and waiting for her by the raspberries. She runs through the kitchen, out the back door and down the garden path, but he isn't there. Chris comes to the door and sees her daughter at the end of the garden, her naked feet dirty and wet.

"Good grief, girl," Chris says. "What are you doing?"

"I thought Daddy was out here," Evelyn says.

"Of course he isn't out here. He's dead," Chris says, and she goes back inside.

After the funeral, Chris's sister, May, offers to take the other two children for the weekend, but she tells Chris that she will have to find somewhere else for Evelyn and Everett to stay. She doesn't say why, but Chris knows that May thinks they are too much like their father, who was mean to May, because he liked beautiful women and May has overdeveloped canines that make her look like a vampire.

Evelyn and Everett are sent to stay with Chris's cousin, whom they are told to call Auntie Doris. Doris has gone to university, and she puts on a posh accent that makes her sound as if she has a cold. She lives with her husband, Noel, an Englishman who came to Maine to start a dairy farm but mostly failed, leaving his family living in a dilapidated house without indoor plumbing.

The children are given a room downstairs, which is damp and musty but close to the wood stove. That night, Evelyn dreams that she is at her father's funeral, and the minister holds his hands over his head and says, "As this man believed in faith healing, God will raise him from the dead like Lazarus." He opens the coffin and Eugene steps out, confectioners' sugar dusting his hair and face.

She wakes up with a warm wetness seeping under her.

"Everett, you're peeing," she says. She shakes him. "Everett," she says louder, and he wakes up. She gets him out of bed and makes him take off his wet pajamas. Auntie Doris is sweeping and Uncle Noel is reading by the fire when Evelyn creeps out of the bedroom.

"What are you doing?" Uncle Noel says.

"Can I have a towel, please," Evelyn says.

"Why?" Uncle Noel says.

"My brother had an accident."

"What do you mean an accident?"

"He wet the bed."

Uncle Noel jumps out of his seat, as if he had been waiting for the news.

"You filthy kid," he shouts at Everett, who is standing by the bed wearing his sister's spare nightgown. "You disgusting filthy kid." Uncle Noel is pulling the sheets off the bed and Everett is shivering, his hands held up to his chest. Uncle Noel thrusts the sheets at him and Everett takes them in his arms. Evelyn stands in the doorway and watches, and after Uncle Noel has finished shouting she helps her brother wash the sheets and his pajamas in a tub of cold water with cheap soap that stains their hands red.

Auntie Doris has remade the bed by the time the children get back to the bedroom. As they slide under the cool new sheets, Everett says, "I dreamt about Daddy."

Evelyn pretends not to hear.

"Evie, I dreamt about Daddy," he says again.

"Go back to sleep," she says.

"Gosh, he was so white in my dream!"

"Hush up, would you?"

"What was he like? Will you tell me?"

"You know him as well as I do," she says, although she knows it isn't true.

"But what was he like when I wasn't there?"

"I don't know."

Everett can always tell with his sister when no means no and when no means keep asking.

"Yes you do. Please tell."

"Okay, he writes lots of songs. He wrote that song about home on the range."

"Sing it to me."

"Home, home on the range," she says.

"Sing it!"

"Where the deer and the antelope play," she sings softly.

"Keep going."

"That's all I know."

"Anyway, I knew that already."

"You asked me to tell you!"

"Tell me what I don't know."

"I don't know what you don't know."

"Do the chewing gum one!" he says.

She sighs. "If I sing it will you go to sleep?"

"Yes."

"If your chewing gum loses its flavour on the bedside overnight, take it to E.I. Ingamels, he'll pretty soon put it right."

"He liked to go to the horse races when Ma thought he was at the shop," Everett says after a few minutes. "He took me sometimes."

"Why?"

"To bet on horses."

"Did he win ever?"

"Sometimes. He had a gun from the war. He let me shoot cans with it."

"Go to sleep," she says.

"Sometimes he took me to hotels and made me wait for him for a long time." Evelyn turns toward the shape of her brother in the dark. "He took me to the shop first and let me fill a bag with anything I wanted."

"What was he doing while you waited?"

"Once I finished a whole gobstopper while I waited for him."

"For him to what?" She can barely see his pale, wet face, and she feels sorry for him, because he is so young and can't understand the things that happen to him.

"He knew lots of ladies," he says.

"Stop making up tales," she says.

"It's not a tale," he says. "One of the ladies was named Mirabel. She was from France and everything."

"Go to sleep," she says, and he can tell this time she means it.

The next morning, Evelyn explores the farm while Everett eats breakfast with Uncle Noel and Auntie Doris. Everyone else seems to have forgotten what happened the night before, but Evelyn refuses to look at Uncle Noel. She goes to the barn to find farm cats to stroke, but she can't catch any. Near the gate at the end of the lane, she sees something moving. When she gets closer, she finds a newborn calf trying to stand up in a metal crate. Hearing her, it stops moving and stares up, keeping its head lowered. She stays very still; after a while it tries again to stand. "There you go," she says. She comes closer and kneels to encourage it. Just as it seems to have its feet under it, a truck comes around the corner, and the startled calf falls back down on the hard metal.

The truck slows and stops. Two men get out. "Good morning," one of them says. "Good morning," Evelyn says. She stands back while they pick up and roughly heave the calf onto the truck's opened gate.

It's then that Evelyn starts to feel sick. As she watches the truck pull away, she vomits on the ground. She makes it to the outhouse before she vomits again. She goes inside the house. Auntie Doris is frying something at the stove, and when she sees Evelyn's face she says, "What's wrong, honey?"

"I'm sick," Evelyn whispers.

"But we're going to the motocross. You won't want to miss that."

Evelyn's stomach is seized with a cramp, and she has to run back outside. No one follows her, so she stays in the outhouse for a long time by herself, trying not to breathe in through her nose or think about the spiders.

An hour later, they leave, including Everett, whose forgetfulness Evelyn has never envied more. He even sits on Uncle Noel's lap in the car. He doesn't know about the calf, so Evelyn forgives him for that.

She goes to the bedroom where Auntie Doris has left her a bucket to vomit in and water to drink. She has to run outside when she starts to have diarrhea, but once it's dark, she can't bring herself to go all the way to the outhouse, so she squats in the garden by the steps. Back inside, lying in the cold bed, she has the darkest feelings of her life. She stares at the mouldy ceiling and remembers with bitterness when the man from the congregational church came to the house to ask Chris to bring the family to the faith healing service. When Chris said no, the man said, "Perhaps we will see you in church when Mr. Ingamels is better."

"You won't ever see my husband or anyone else from this family in your church," Chris said. She was right, Evelyn thinks. He didn't go to their church, and he didn't get better, either.

She allows herself to really think about him for the first time. She pictures his face. Blue eyes, hard skin creased like a pie shell, coarse hands. She thinks about the nights he held her and sang her to sleep—only her, never the others. She imagines him stroking her hair, telling her that he will always love her best. She imagines him with those women Everett talked about, with Mirabel, and then she says *He's dead he's dead he's dead* until she feels some strange relief and finally falls asleep.

*

Thirty years later, Evelyn is recovering after having her gallbladder out. It's Sunday, and her husband has taken the children to a park where they're going to ride boats while she stays home in bed. It was her idea that they should go, because the kids haven't had much of a summer, but now that they are gone she feels unaccountably betrayed, and she lies awake in bed thinking spiteful thoughts about all of them.

When she finally manages to fall asleep, she has the recurring dream in which she receives a letter from her father. *Now that your mother is dead, I can let you know that I'm alive*, he writes. *I couldn't stand living with her any more, but a divorce would have been a disgrace, so I worked out this trick with my Auntie Evelyn from England, who I told you about, and now I live here with her and we want you to join us!*

At the bottom of the letter is his address in England and enough money for her passage. She packs and runs to the docks, but once she's aboard the ship, she realizes her things have been taken out of her suitcase and thrown among piles of discarded junk. She runs desperately through the bowels of the ship, through the sleeping quarters and the dining room, collecting her stuff. Once she's on the top deck again, she looks to see if her father is waiting for her on the wharf, but there is no wharf, just a patch of grass with a hut on it, dwarfed by an everlasting forest. There is no one there to meet her, and she has lost the letter with the address on it. It's the most important thing, and now she will never know. It's the key to her life, and it's gone.

She wakes up cold, hungry and in pain. She calls to her husband but no one answers. She expects that he will be home any minute, and she plans to tell him about her dream and to cry, even though it's not the dream that's upset her. By the time he does get home, well after dark, Evelyn is hysterical. He says she's being ridiculous, and she says she felt totally abandoned. He's angry and tells her she has a victim mentality and to stop being so melodramatic.

Years later, one of Evelyn's sons casually mentions over lunch that the woman his father left her for was in the rented boats with them that afternoon. Evelyn's husband had introduced the woman to his children as a friend from work, and after the boats he'd taken them to her house and left them to play with her sons. As Evelyn eats her tuna sandwich, she pictures the woman with her family that day, sitting low in the hull, drawing her hand through the water and singing while Evelyn's husband pulls on the oars.

1890
The Solomon Vale

THE MAN HAD A GUITAR and the sweetest voice anyone had ever heard, so they let him sing for a while before they asked who he was and what he was doing in their kitchen. He said he was on his way to California and asked if they would be willing to let him stay for a night or two. Ida said he shouldn't have soaked her floor with his wet boots, but Henrick said they couldn't put him out in the cold, and it would be fine so long as he put in a day's work and didn't mind playing some more.

In the kitchen that night there were Ida and Henrick De Jong, whose house it was, and Henrick's brother Bram De Jong, plus Walter Finch and some men who worked for him, and George Craven and his eldest son, William. The De Jong children were lying awake in bed, listening to the sounds below. The eldest, Florence, recognized some of the songs the stranger was singing, but mostly he played old gold mining tunes and cowboy hymns that she didn't know.

After a while, the man stopped playing and talked a bit. He

said his name was Alphonse.

"Why do you want to go to California in the middle of winter?" Henrick asked him.

The man looked down at his hands. "I've been on my way there for some time, but I never seem to make it," he said.

"It's the same with me," said Henrick.

"What're you going to do when you do get there?" George Craven asked.

The man looked up at Henrick, ignoring George's question. "You a farmer?" he said.

"Yes," Henrick said.

"I always wanted to be a farmer," the man said, and then he cocked his head to the side as if speaking to a copy of himself. "What do you do, Alphonse?" he said to the place where his head used to be, and then turning back in the other direction, he answered himself, "I'm a farmer." He laughed at his joke, so the men laughed too, but they all thought it was strange, and from her bedroom Florence thought so as well.

"You all farmers?" the man asked.

"Except George. He works for the county."

"Doin' what?"

"Surveying," George answered, without warmth.

The man was clearly impressed. "I tell you, I've always had an interest in surveying. Ever since I was a boy I was interested in that work. How you like it?"

"I like it fine."

"Well, we should go into business," the man said. "You seem like good people, and I got some capital I'm hoping to invest from my prospecting days. I'm waiting for the right opportunity, you know?"

"Why don't you play some more?" Henrick said, not liking the way things were turning.

"You know 'Sweet Betsy from Pike'?" asked William.

"No," said the man, "but I know a song about her." He began to sing again, and so sang Florence to sleep.

The next morning the man was gone, and Henrick checked his hiding place to find his pocket watch gone too. That was the watch his father had given him, which had been given to him by *his* father, who had died within a week of arriving in America. He checked the barn. His horse was missing, and in its place was the man's bony mare. He told Ida and the children to stay inside while he rode Ida's horse to Bram's farm.

Bram and Walter were standing by the barn. Henrick's horse was tied up next to them. When they saw Henrick coming, Bram held his finger to his lips, and Henrick slowed to a walk until he was within earshot. Before he could ask what was going on, Bram pointed to the barn. "He's sleeping in the haystack," he said.

"Cunt stole grandfather's watch," said Henrick, who seldom cussed. He tied Ida's horse next to the horse the man had stolen and walked through the thin snow toward the barn, followed by Bram and Walter.

"What're you going to do?" Walter said, but Henrick ignored him. The man was asleep, cradling his guitar in his arms. When Henrick was within a few metres of him, the man woke up and held out his hands to defend himself. His guitar slid down the haystack to land on the floor with a discordant sound. "Careful," he said

"You cocksucker," said Henrick. "You devil."

"What, what?" the man said. "What I do?"

"Hold him," Henrick said, and he looked around the barn for some rope. Bram held the man's arms and Walter put a foot on his chest. The man didn't try to get up, only kept asking what he'd done and what they wanted.

"Please tell me what happened," he said as Henrick started to tie him. "I swear I don't remember nothin'. Did I do something bad?"

"Shut your mouth," Henrick said. "I knew there was something wrong with you the second I laid eyes on you. Why I didn't do something about it then I don't know. Should've thrown you out in the snow, walking into my house like that."

"Listen," the man said. "I'm sorry. I should'a asked before coming in. There was a lot of people though, and I was cold. I thought you liked my playin'."

"You chose the wrong man to steal from," Henrick said.

"What?" the man said. "I never…unless…is it your horse?" He tried to peer outside, but Walter pushed him down with his boot.

"Stop talking," Henrick said.

Henrick bound the man's hands and legs before tying him to the bars of a stall. The man kept talking, saying how he had started drinking after they went to bed and he couldn't remember much when he was drinking, but no harm done because the horse must be there outside, and who didn't make a mistake every now and then when they'd had too much to drink?

When he'd finished tying the man, Henrick left him with Walter while he went into the house, followed by Bram.

"Where do you keep your razor?" Henrick said.

Bram's wife and baby were sitting in the rocker by the door, but she didn't look up, not wanting to get involved in a fight between the brothers.

"Come on, Henrick," Bram said. "We'll get the watch back. Where can he have hidden it?"

"It's not about the watch," Henrick shouted, and Bram's baby started to cry. "It's about respect, goddamn it. You don't walk into a man's house and take his hospitality and then help yourself to whatever you want. We can't let him get away with it."

"Agreed," said Bram, "but you can't kill him."

When they got back, Walter was standing outside of the barn. "I didn't want to listen to him no more," he said. When he saw the razor in Henrick's hand he said, "What're you gonna do?"

In the barn, Henrick took an old saddle blanket from a stall and shoved a corner into the man's mouth. "We're going to give this fellow a haircut," he said. He broke through the ice on the trough to collect some water in a pail. He poured the freezing water over the man's head, and the man screamed. He directed Bram and Walter to hold the man's head still while he shaved off the greasy brown hair on the left side and the beard and eyebrow on the right, leaving a rough, bloody mess. When he had finished, Henrick removed the man's gag.

"Now where's my grandfather's watch?"

"What?" the man said. "I don't know what you're talkin' about." He had bitten himself in his struggle, and when he spoke blood and spit sprayed from his mouth.

"I guess you aren't happy with your haircut," Henrick said. "You want some more off the top?"

"Fuck you!" the man said.

Henrick reopened his razor. The man continued to bawl and protest as Henrick held his head to the side and cut through his ear, making a clean horizontal slice through the cartilage. After that, they searched the man's clothes thoroughly before leaving him alone in the barn.

Walter offered that if they could find out where he had hidden the watch it would be all right and they could let him go. Henrick didn't respond. When they came back into the barn, the man was staring off into the distance behind them. Walter roughly prodded him with the toe of his boot. "We're gonna let you go," he said. "But we don't ever want to see you around here again. Understand?"

"Yes," the man said. "I'll never come back here again. I promise. And I didn't take no watch. I'll promise that too."

"You're not going anywhere until you tell us where it is," Henrick said.

"I told you, I ain't took no watch."

Henrick went to the spot where the man had slept, picked up his guitar and held it over his head by the neck as if it were a living thing he meant to brain against the wall.

"Please," the man said. "I promise I didn't take your watch. I don't even know how to tell time, what use I got for a watch?"

"Last chance," Henrick said.

"Please," the man said once more.

Henrick smashed the guitar against the bars of a stall, breaking its back, then took it by the neck and cracked it over his knee.

They rode with the man to Henrick's house to get his horse. He was silent the whole way, not looking at any of them, the blood from his ear frozen on the side of his face. When Ida saw him, she felt terribly afraid, so against her husband's wishes she gave him some food and made him a bandage from an old dress. She stood behind Henrick as the man silently mounted his horse and left. The two of them watched, Ida peering out from behind her husband, until the man had disappeared among the trees.

Three days later, Henrick was walking across the frozen creek on his way back from Walter's house. He sang to himself and occasionally ran a few steps then slid on the ice. He had just completed a series of three running slides when he was hit from behind with a wooden fence post. Some barb sliced through his nose when the post came down on him a second time. He lay still but conscious on the ice.

The man's hair was cropped shorter on the right side now, but the left was still patchy and scabbed, his beard motley and spotted with blood. Filthy shreds of a woman's dress blew around his ear. He brought his face close to Henrick's ruined nose, and steam rose around him as he hissed, "I could'a screwed your wife, I could'a screwed them kids you got, I didn't do none of that, only accidentally took your horse 'stead of my own on account of I was drunk and didn't know what I was doin'. I could'a screwed that little girl you got, but I didn't do nothing, I left her lyin' there sleepin'. And you bastards come after me talkin' about I took a watch. I never took no watch. I been blamed my whole life for shit I didn't do. I'm sick to death of it."

He raised the fence post again and continued to beat Henrick until he was dead or unconscious. Then he used the post to make a hole in the ice to push Henrick's body through.

In the spring, Henrick's body was found half buried in the slimy grass along the edge of the creek. Everyone assumed it was the strange man who had killed him, but there was nothing to be done. It wasn't until ten years later that it came clear. A man in Wyoming had been sentenced to hanging for beating his wife so badly she ran outside to get away from him and froze to death. When he was up on the gallows, he admitted to killing a man named De Jong some years earlier. He said that they were business partners, and they'd had a dispute over an investment. By the time the De Jongs found out, it was too late for the pleasure of vengeance or even much grief. They were used to it now.

"I guess he never got to California," was all Bram said when he heard the news.

1928
Medicine Song

THE FIRST TIME I HEARD ABOUT FRANK I was at the Farmer Street greengrocers, where I worked after school and on Friday nights. Julia Keyes and Carolyn Kenney came in and started raving about this man they had met, telling me how handsome and sophisticated he was, how he had travelled in Europe and gone to university in Italy and how he used to sing in a nightclub in New York. Julia said, "He's a great lover," and I couldn't hide my shock. Neither could Carolyn, because she had been intimate with him too, but she got over it, and they both seemed to decide that it was even more sophisticated like that.

I felt sorry for them, because I thought they weren't as clever as me and didn't know that you had to stay a virgin if you wanted to marry someone good. I still enjoyed having them as friends, though, because there were three of us, so whenever I didn't want to do something I didn't have to worry about either of them being alone. That was important, because I often didn't want to do what they were doing. I wasn't allowed to go dancing, for one thing, because my father thought it was sinful, and I certainly had no interest in drinking alcohol or having sex with boys, activities which my two friends couldn't stop talking about. Most of my socializing took place in Bible class, and the only music I knew was religious. I loved to sing, and I knew every hymn in the hymnal by heart. The summer before, I had gone to Easter camp and won the music competition for singing "The Old Rugged Cross," which was my favourite hymn at the time.

One day Julia and Carolyn came into the greengrocers with Frank. He was wearing a black cape with red lining and carrying a walking stick with a carved ivory head. He had dark curly hair, and although he wasn't tall, he was certainly unusual. What I mean is, he had oddity value, especially for Tempe.

Frank removed a glove before introducing himself and shaking my hand. Then he turned to Julia and said, "She's a beauty, isn't she?" as if I wasn't even there. It was nice to get a bit of encouragement about myself, since I had spent so much of my life being reminded of my faults. And it was true what he said. I was very beautiful, even if I did wear my hair like a nun.

Frank looked at me strangely then.

"Have we met before?" he said. I told him we hadn't. "But I know you," he said.

"No you don't," I said. I thought it must be something he liked to say to girls.

He was singing at a place not far from there, and he asked if I would come. I said my father wouldn't allow it, but Frank promised that he would get me home before nine. I guess I felt afraid of missing out on something, and I was also starting to think about trying to rebel against my father a bit, so I agreed to go.

The place was a dingy old room at the back of a house on the outskirts of town. A guy named Jazz Foot played the drums in Frank's band, and I thought it was a beautiful name and didn't realize he had made it up. Roger was the weedy one who played the guitar. The saxophone player called himself Chicken. Frank played the other guitar and sang. At one point he sang "My Love is Like a Red, Red Rose," and he stared at me the whole time. I felt so awkward in my shop uniform with everyone looking at me. When the song was over, he came off the stage, sat next to me and took my hands in his.

"Were you in a parade in Phoenix two years ago?" he said. I didn't have to think about it. It was the only parade I'd ever been in. Some woman from the church was organizing a float and she wanted me to be an Irish princess. I wore a green tartan dress and sat at the front pretending to play a harp. My father agreed to it without even asking me first, because that woman was quite important in the community.

"I was there," he said. "I remember you."

Carolyn and Julia were listening too. Carolyn leaned over and said, "You remember her from two years ago? That's amazing!"

"Look at those eyes," he said, holding his hand up next to my face. "How could I forget them?"

He drove me home in a red sports car that belonged to Julia Keyes's father. He insisted that I sit beside him, and he made

Julia and Carolyn sit in the back. Those girls didn't have much self-respect, because it seemed like the meaner he was to them, the more they loved him. When he dropped me off, he asked when he would see me again. I said I didn't know and ran inside.

After that, Frank continued to pursue me. He would come into the shop and wait so that I would have to serve him. He would buy one thing, like an apple or a pound of carrots, and try to start a conversation with me, and I would have to tell him I was too busy to talk. He often waited for me to finish work, and then he would walk me home and talk to me about all sorts of things. He would tell me about places he had been in Europe, about magnificent cathedrals and choirs singing in hillside towns and the Eiffel Tower in Paris and the Coliseum in Rome. He told me he would take me there someday, and I would see all of those things.

I told Frank I would never be his girlfriend, because he was not my type of person. He asked what I meant, and I told him it was because he wasn't a Christian. He said he was an Anglican, but I knew he was an atheist because he had already let that slip. He'd been brought up Anglican, but his parents had stopped going to church when he was a teenager. He told me that as a child he sang in the church choir, and he took money out of the collection plates instead of putting it in. I wondered why he would tell me that when he knew how I was.

Finally Frank pressed me so much that I told him I knew he had slept with my friends. I thought he would be embarrassed, but he seemed confused and said, "So what? That was before I met you." He asked if I was a virgin, and I said of course

I was, and he said how odd. I said it's actually very common among people who have morals, and then I turned away from him and ran home.

The next day he was back at the greengrocers. He told me he was sorry and asked if I would like to go to church with him on Sunday. I thought I might be having a good influence on him, so I said yes. That Sunday I told my father I would be going with a friend to another Baptist church in Phoenix. Frank met me outside my work, as we had arranged, and to my surprise he had his parents with him in Julia Keyes's father's car.

"This is my father, William," Frank said. "You can call him Pop."

"Pleased to meet you," I said, and I curtsied, because I thought it was the appropriate thing to do.

"Look at those eyes. My God, that's trouble," Pop said.

Frank's mother, Mary, barely talked to me at all, but Pop wouldn't leave me alone. After the service—which wasn't very different from what I was used to, despite what my father had led me to believe about Anglicans—we went back to Pop and Mary's farm for lunch. Pop gave me seltzer water in a wine glass, and I thought what I was doing was so much more mature than sitting in a car letting some teenage boy put his germy mouth all over me like Julia and Carolyn probably were. While I was drinking my seltzer water, Mary got up to peel vegetables and Frank went to the piano and started to play. Mary was humming along, and then Pop came in with his violin and joined Frank, and Frank joined Mary in singing, and the whole time I couldn't stop watching Frank's hands on the keys.

I hadn't realized until that day that Frank lived with his parents. In fact, I had never thought about where he might live. If I had, I probably would have pictured him in some seedy apartment or the crypt of a church or something. But Pop and Mary's farmhouse was bright and clean, filled with the kinds of things that people living in the same place for generations accumulate. Down by the chicken coop they had a well that was the deepest around, and they gave the water away to anyone who wanted it, even though it cost them to pump it with the gasoline engine. Seeing that farm made me consider Frank differently, even if the only thing his parents raised were a few chickens and a fat old pig they couldn't bring themselves to slaughter.

While we were eating lunch, Pop said, "I'm so glad Frank found you." I asked him what he meant.

"Didn't he tell you that we saw you in Phoenix two years ago?" Pop said.

"Oh, yes," I said.

"And isn't it amazing?"

"I suppose." I could feel Frank staring at me from across the table.

"He might not want me to tell you this, but at the time he said to me, 'That's the girl I'm going to marry. That's my wife up there.' He really did a lot to try and find out who you were."

I could feel all three of them watching me, waiting to see how I would react, but I kept my head lowered and tried to think of ways to change the topic. I had been so sure that I couldn't be with Frank, but to have someone be that certain about you is a powerful thing, because if you won't believe in someone else's destiny, you can't really believe in your own, and I very much wanted to believe that I had a destiny, even though I had no idea what it might be.

I started to spend more and more time with Frank at his parents' house, telling my father that I was working longer hours at the greengrocers to save money for nursing school. We would spend hours singing old hymns, and I was impressed with how many of the best ones they knew. They also played songs they had written together, some of them very good.

Sometimes they took me out to the roller rink or the cinema, both of which they owned, and Pop instructed the concession stand girls to give me anything I wanted. The cinema had originally been an opera house, and Mary had been the star, but they couldn't make enough money in a place like Tempe, so they'd had to convert it. Pop was the projectionist. I sat in the booth next to him and watched the movie through the dusty glass, and between reels Mary would get up and sing arias for the audience.

Often in the afternoon Pop would sit on the sofa with Mary, brushing her hair. And when people came to get water and stayed too long, Pop handed them their hats and said, "Here's your hat, what's your hurry?" But he always did it in such a nice way, you couldn't mind. He was as bad as Frank for telling me stories about places I would never see, but he hadn't been to Europe like Frank, so instead he told me about things from his youth, like seeing Sitting Bull at Buffalo Bill's Wild West, or playing violin at a school fair that was attended by Ulysses S. Grant.

Things continued like that for some time, until one day my father came to the greengrocers looking for me and I wasn't there. When I got home, he asked where I had been, and when I told him I had been at work he flew into a rage and said that I was a sinful child and a liar and that I had the devil in me. I was sick of lying to him by then, so I told him I had met a young man and I had been spending time with his family, getting to know them better.

"What are this person's intentions?" he asked.

"He doesn't expect anything from me," I said. "He's happy that I'm a virgin."

That was a mistake. My father's face twitched and he made his hands into fists.

"Who does this person think he is, asking a young schoolgirl about her virginity?"

"Calm down," I said.

"Don't tell me to calm down," he said. "Is he a Baptist?"

"He's Anglican," I said, hoping that Frank being a Christian would be enough.

"What? What are you doing with an Anglican, girl? Don't you know how misguided they are? And why wouldn't this person come and meet your parents instead of sneaking around with you like a criminal?"

I told Frank he had to come and meet my father if he wanted to keep seeing me. Two days later, he pulled into my parents' driveway in Julia Keyes's father's car. He was wearing a suit and tie, and he came in and did a whole song and dance for my parents. He put on a strange accent and talked about how he had gone to university in Italy and how he was planning to begin medical school in the fall, which was the first I'd heard of it.

I watched his performance with a growing sense of horror. My father's face was getting redder and redder, but Frank didn't even notice what was happening until my father said, "Leave this house immediately and don't ever speak to my daughter again or I'll call the police." He picked up the fire poker and started chasing Frank with it. Frank got out of there as fast as he could, and my father said that if I ever saw Frank again, he would disown me.

If I had been left to make my own choice, it probably wouldn't have taken me long to see that Frank wasn't suitable. As it was, my father's ultimatum told me that his ideas about right and wrong meant more to him than I did, and realizing that made me determined to find out if there was a better kind of love out there for me.

I went to Pop and Mary's house and told Pop what had happened, and he said I could stay there as long as I wanted. I stayed with them until I had finished my final exams for high school, and then I applied to nursing school. During that time I had contact with my mother, but my father refused to speak to me. I suppose he was trying to make me regret my decision, but in fact the effect was the opposite.

The college I had applied to was in Phoenix, so I went and stayed with my mother's brother, Hugh, and got a job as a filing clerk while I waited to find out if I had been accepted. Before I left, Frank sat me down and asked very sincerely if I would consider marrying him and getting the farm going again. I laughed because I thought he couldn't be serious and it was so funny to imagine Frank working on a farm.

After I moved to Phoenix, Frank and Pop would come and visit me on the weekends and take me out to hear music. Pop was always the oldest person in the place, but he never seemed to mind. It occurred to me that Pop wanted to be Frank in a way, but that was hard, because pretty soon I started to realize that Frank wanted to be somebody different every week.

When I found out I had been accepted to college, I decided to stay living with my uncle Hugh. I had begun to imagine myself as old, even though I was the youngest in my class. I didn't think I could fit in with the girls in the dormitory, since I couldn't bring myself to join in with the dancing and backseat petting and silly sports games and all that. So I stayed with my uncle, and Pop and Frank started coming up to see me during the week. Finally they got an apartment not far from where I lived and they started living there about half the time. I never got to ask what Mary thought about this arrangement, because I never saw her any more, but Pop and Frank both seemed pretty happy about it.

Frank got a day job driving a truck for the disabled citizens and another job playing music two nights a week. Pop started taking some art classes at the Lions Club, and Frank had parties at their house almost every weekend, although I didn't go, because I never touched alcohol in those days, and I hated to see people drunk. Sometimes I wondered what went on at those parties. I knew that Frank had plenty of women who wanted to be with him, and I knew that he fed off that, but I told myself that if he wanted to be with them, he wouldn't keep pursuing me.

One night I went with Pop to a club where Frank and his band were playing. I was sitting with Pop in a booth, drinking my soda. Pop kept ordering drinks for himself and the people around us, and I thought we were having a nice time, but I noticed Pop seemed sad.

"What's wrong?" I said.

"Don't worry about me, blossom," he said. "Nothing's gonna kill me. You can't kill weeds." I left it at that, and after a while he said, "I always thought I would be famous, you know? Everyone always said I had so much promise as a musician when I was younger, but it didn't go anywhere." He reached out and grabbed my breast. I was so shocked that I couldn't say anything. I pulled away, and he took his hand back and looked at the band and kept snapping his fingers to the music like nothing had happened, but I felt sick about it.

Frank and I had to carry Pop home because he was so drunk, and when we got there Pop went to his room and started having a fit about how there were infidels in the mirror and in the books, and he was fighting a holy war against them. I tried to calm him down, but Frank walked away. Then Pop started throwing all the things in his room out the window. The furniture, his clothing. He didn't stop until everything was gone except his mattress, and then he went to sleep on it.

Once Pop was asleep, I went looking for Frank. I found him in the kitchen eating plain bread, and crying. I had never seen him cry before. I asked him what was wrong, and he told me that he had a malignant growth in his testicle—he didn't say cancer—and he was going to have an operation. I stayed with him that night and slept next to him in his bed. The next day I missed my classes in order to help Pop get his room back together. Some of his things had been taken, and others were too broken to fix, but we pulled things together as much as possible and at least made the room livable again.

When I left their apartment that day I felt so sorry for those two. Sorry and also responsible. I think I decided that it was my job to take care of them, and once I'd decided that, I couldn't take it back. It was very frightening, because all my former certainties were sort of dissolving, and I knew that was a dangerous way to live, because you might do anything at all.

I stayed on and helped Frank and Pop around the house and tried to make them cheerful as much as I could. Then the day of Frank's operation came. I had an exam at school, so I went there and wrote the exam, completely pulling everything out of thin air, and then I went to the hospital. When I arrived, Frank was in bed, hooked up to tubes, and Pop was sitting next to him. I could tell that Pop had been crying.

"Do you know what would make Frank happier than anything in the world?" he said when he saw me. I asked what and he said, "If you would marry him."

I was so young that I had to get my parents' consent to marry, which meant I had to face my father for the first time since that terrible day when he first met Frank. He said he would never consent to my marrying an Anglican who had one foot in the grave, but when I told him I would get pregnant if he didn't agree, he changed his tune. I suppose he'd given up on me, and he thought it would be better to have me married in the Baptist church than living in sin. For me I think the marriage was a safety measure. Once I'd decided that it was my job to take care of Frank, I wanted to make sure I was in good with God, because I needed a miracle.

People at the wedding knew that Frank was sick, but they

didn't know how serious it was. Even those among us who did know didn't admit it to ourselves. We had been told that we had to wait and find out if the cancer had spread, so there was nothing else to do. I was surprised by how easy I found it to forget about all of that on my wedding day. We had arranged to get married quite quickly, and Pop spared no expense. I had the most beautiful white silk dress, and Julia and Carolyn were my bridesmaids. We had a wedding reception at a chalet, and my father wanted to have raspberry drink only, but Pop snuck in rum and beer.

I loved my wedding. It was so much fun being the centre of attention, and I wasn't even bothered by the terrible wedding presents. Mary gave Frank a pair of shoes, and at the time I thought it was because she didn't want him to marry me. Pop bought us a hunting rifle. My father gave us an engraved Bible. A man named Andrew Smith, who was Pop and Mary's former accountant, gave us a set of steak knives, but those went into the garbage. Later I discovered that that man had interfered with Frank when Frank was a child, but at the time I just thought that the knives were ugly.

After the reception, when we were alone in our room, Frank stood behind me in front of the full-length mirror. We were still in our wedding clothes, and I remember looking at his face and feeling that I didn't recognize him. As I watched him unbutton the back of my dress, I had the unsettling impression that I was looking at a stranger, and I felt how terribly odd and even embarrassing it was to be married to someone you didn't know.

"I can't believe it's happened," he said, running his hands along the arms and bodice of my dress. I smiled bravely and raised his hand to my lips to kiss it, telling myself that of course I knew him. "You were wearing white the first time I saw you," he said. "Do you remember?"

"My uniform was blue," I said, thinking that he must have meant when we met at the greengrocers.

"No, silly. In the parade." He caressed my hair. "You had flowers in your hair, and you wore a long white dress. You were the most beautiful thing I could imagine. It was like I had invented you. And did I ever tell you how hard I tried to find out who you were?" I had started to cry, because then I knew that it wasn't me he'd seen at all. He thought I was moved by what he was telling me, and he made small sounds of comfort as he kissed my neck and carried me to the bed.

After that, I moved into Pop and Frank's apartment with them, and Pop almost never went home to Mary any more. It was just the three of us living there together, and most people thought Pop was a widower and Frank and I were taking care of him. I stayed home with Frank, and Pop started doing Frank's runs to pick up the disabled citizens. Frank would send him out every day with a list of the things he wanted, like rum or cigarettes, and even though Frank wasn't supposed to have any of those things, Pop would always get them. Sometimes Pop came home with beautiful presents for me or for the house, and I couldn't bring myself to tell him that we needed to save our money.

It was during that time that I became pregnant. Frank's doctor had said it would be impossible for us to conceive a child because of Frank's treatment, and when I told him that I was pregnant, he referred me to someone who would give me an abortion, because he said there was almost no chance that the baby would be normal. I never considered doing it, though. I believed everything would be fine.

Frank and Pop were completely overjoyed. I telephoned Mary to tell her, and she offered to come and stay with us at the apartment if we needed her, which meant a lot to me. When I told my own mother, she said, "Oh my God, are you insane?" But I didn't mind much what my parents thought by then.

For the first while, I was very sick all the time, and eventually I got so thin that my wedding ring fell off. Frank also got more and more thin, so we were wasting away in that house, but at least our food bills were cheap. Then Frank had to have another operation to have secondary cancers that had appeared in his lungs removed. Pop and I went with him, and after we had waited in the hall for what seemed like an eternity, the surgeon called us into his office. He told us very matter-of-factly that he was sorry, but the cancer had spread too much, and Frank probably only had about six weeks left. It crossed my mind that this was an unfair punishment for disobeying my father, but then I chastised myself for thinking it, because it wasn't about me at all.

The doctor told Frank his prognosis while Pop and I waited outside. When the doctor came out, we went into the room and Pop told Frank not to worry because he would make sure the baby was taken care of and he would be like a father to it. Then the specialist came in and asked if he could have a word with us. He said that throughout his career he had, time and time again, seen people go home riddled with cancer and come back in complete remission, and even though he wasn't a religious person, the only explanation he could come up with was that God had a hand in it, because what all those people had in common was that they went to faith healing.

The next day, I started looking for a church that would do faith healing services, and once I found one, I had another job to convince Frank to come with me. In the end, he accepted that he had nothing to lose from it, so he came, and Pop came too. It was a tiny church with only two windows, and the preacher was an Englishman who seemed very proper until he pulled out his banjo and started singing, which made me love him. After the service, he came over to us and said, "I have this strong feeling about you people, and I believe that you came here for a reason." I told him everything, and he said we should come back the next week and he would perform a healing service for us.

Pop, Mary and some of their friends came with us to the church for the service. The preacher had arranged everything, and he had invited his parishioners to support us as well. The service was short. The preacher said, "Are any sick among you?" and Frank stood up. The preacher said, "Let him call for the elders of the church, and let them pray over him, anointing him with oil in the name of the Lord." He led Frank to the front of the church and asked him to kneel while he made the sign of the cross in oil on his forehead. As he did this, he said "And the prayer of faith shall save the sick, and the Lord shall raise him up."

He turned to the congregation, and in unison they said, "In the name of Christ the great physician, we command this person to be well."

After that the preacher got out his banjo and we all sang "There is Healing in His Name," and some of the parishioners started to speak in tongues and some fell to the ground. I had never seen anything like it in my life, and I didn't know why but I couldn't stop crying. I cried throughout the whole thing and all the way home and all the rest of the night. I thought I might never stop, but eventually I did, and I slept for two whole days.

Theresa was born with lots of black hair and slanted eyes, and she was a bit yellow from being jaundiced. I thought she was the most gorgeous thing I had ever seen. As soon as he was allowed, Pop came into the room and washed his hands and said, "Where's my baby?" and he wouldn't let Theresa go once he got hold of her. He always did love her more than Frank did, from the very first day.

There was a girl in the hospital that I had gone to school with. Her name was Laura, and she also had a new baby, and we joked about how funny it was, us living parallel lives, but then we found out that Laura's baby had bone cancer. I told Laura about Frank's faith healing, and once we were out of the hospital I went to the church with her to do a service for the baby. After that, Laura became enmeshed in our lives and ended up living in our house with us, because she wanted to leave her husband, who beat her up. I later saw what a mistake that was, but I wasn't very good at putting up boundaries around myself in those days, and neither was Frank.

By that time, Frank had lived three months longer than he was supposed to, and he was healthier than ever. The doctors were amazed, of course, but nothing amazed me any more. I was going to church again, to the same church where Frank had been healed, and I had already participated in healing services for four other people. Frank always said he would go, but when the time came he was too busy.

He had decided he wanted to move us all to New York so that he could get his singing career going again, but he needed money to do it, because he had spent all of his and Pop's when he thought he was going to die. In order to get some cash, he and Pop started an antiques business. They used the truck from the disabled citizens to drive around to people's homes and buy their antiques for next to nothing. They would put a bit of polish on them and sell them in their store for five times more than they had paid. They didn't care if they got a bad reputation for doing it, because they were planning to leave anyway. I didn't say anything, because I believed that God must have let Frank live for a reason, and it wasn't my place to judge.

The only thing I did get upset with him about was the incident with the violin. One day, two women brought a violin into the shop. They said it had belonged to their grandfather, and they wanted to know what it was worth. Frank told them it wasn't very valuable, and they sold it to him for a pittance. I watched the whole exchange, and I thought how sad it was that those women were desperate enough to sell their grandfather's violin.

As soon as they were gone, Frank was on the phone calling around about this thing, because apparently it was worth quite a lot of money and he had known it all along. The next day, the women came back and they said they regretted what they had done and it broke their mother's heart when she found out about it. They asked to buy the violin back, but Frank said no. It was the coldest thing I had seen in my life. He said, "Sorry ladies. A deal's a deal." Then he turned over the "Closed" sign on the door. I thought it was beastly of him, and I told him so, but it made no difference.

After a while, Frank and Pop got tired of haggling with people over their furniture, so they started breaking into empty homes and taking what they liked. Sometimes they needed help, because Pop was an old man, and I tried not to get involved, except once I helped them take some brass beds that were in a barn. I told Frank not to do that breaking-in business, but he didn't listen to me at all any more. Once he brought home a doll for Theresa that had a big burn mark on its hand. Another time he brought me a brooch with three rubies and a hole where a fourth was supposed to be, but I told him I didn't want it. He was trying to make up for selling some of my things, including a ring that my grandmother had given me, but I forgave him in the end, because I figured that I didn't know what it was like to almost die.

It was a similar feeling that stopped me from reacting when I found Frank in bed with Laura. I closed the door and walked away, but I told myself that one day he wouldn't be my husband any more.

Soon Frank lost all interest in music, and he became meaner every day. Once he hit Pop because Pop wouldn't give him money. I suspected that he and Laura were bootlegging, but I knew there was nothing I could do to stop him. I wished he would live a better life, because God had saved him and he owed it to God, but after a while I stopped caring what kind of life he lived.

Pop kept living in the apartment with Frank and Laura, but Theresa and I moved back to my uncle Hugh's house. Shortly after that, Laura got caught shoplifting, but they let her off because her baby had died. Mary sent me a letter and asked if I would like to come back to Tempe and live with her, and I had to tell her that I couldn't. I thought people must gossip about me back home. To come back with a young child and without my husband didn't seem fair to my father. Instead I contacted the nursing school and I told them what had happened, focusing on the parts about the miraculous pregnancy and the miraculous recovery and leaving out the parts about the stealing and infidelity and impending divorce. They told me they had tried to contact me after that last exam I wrote, because I had the best mark in the class and the dean wanted to meet me. Then I knew that school was a waste of time, but I went back anyhow, and Pop and Mary helped me to take care of Theresa while I finished my program and became a nurse, which was what I had always wanted to do.

Theresa continued to think of Frank as her father, even after I remarried. Pop hears from Frank every now and then, and he always passes on the news. When Pop and Mary were involved in that terrible lawsuit about that song they wrote, Frank came home for a while, but once things settled down he was off again, taking whatever money they had with him. The last we heard, he was working on an asparagus farm in California, and he had some young girlfriend living with him.

You can spend a lot of time being angry. I was angry with Frank and angry with God and angry about how little sense it all made. I wanted to feel the certainty I knew when I was a child in my father's house and that I had briefly felt again after Frank was healed, but it never came back. Sometimes I have glimpses of it, but it doesn't last.

I still wonder why God saved Frank instead of Laura's baby, or Mary, who died recently, but then I remind myself of something that Mary said while she was in hospital. I was visiting her, and we were doing the crossword puzzle together in her room, when out of the blue she said that she would like to go home. At first I thought she meant heaven, but then she said, "I want to hug my house. To say goodbye." It touched me to hear her say that, because she was not a sentimental person. Then she said, "You know, everything I thought was so important in life was just a joke." At the time I didn't like her saying that, but now I think I understand what she meant.

1908
Seeing the Elephant

WHEN A WESTERNER TALKS about "seeing the elephant," he means having an experience that changes his life forever. John had seen an elephant once, but it hadn't changed his life. When he was a child in Bosque County, the circus had passed along the part of the Chisholm Trail that ran by his father's ranch. There were camels and cages, a calliope painted with stars and stripes pulled by two white horses, and an elephant draped in red velvet led it all.

The trail had brought so many strange creatures to John's front door that he simply took the elephant for another and wondered what would come next. It was Nat, the Negro who worked for John's father, who really saw that elephant. Later that day, Nat set up a trapeze between two oak trees, and from then on he tried unceasingly to convince John and his brothers to spend their work breaks making human pyramids, turning somersaults and handsprings or attempting terrifying flips and contortions.

Arriving at The White Elephant in Fort Worth, Texas, John thought of Nat singing "The Camptown Races" as he balanced one-legged on the bare back of his cantering pony. "I went down there with my hat caved in," John sang to himself under his breath as he approached the saloon. "I came back home with a pocket full of tin." A liveried doorman held open the saloon door, which was a relief, since John was fed up with trying to get his Ediphone safely through doors without losing some part of either the machine or his dignity in the process.

Inside, the place was more elegant than he had expected, with bevelled mirrors, finely carved wooden furniture and crystal chandeliers. Hundreds of cowboy hats hung upside down from the ceiling. The proprietor spoke from behind the filigreed mahogany bar.

"I've been watching you all the way from your automobile," the man said. "What is that thing?" John set the device down and straightened himself out.

"This is an Edison recording device. I'm a professor from Harvard University, and I'm collecting frontier ballads for a book." He was a professor, and he was there on behalf of Harvard, so this wasn't entirely untrue.

"Bring it around here," the proprietor said.

"I hope you won't think I'm rude, but I wonder if you know anyone who might be familiar with some of the old songs."

Three cowboys, two young and one old, were playing penny-ante poker at a table in the far corner. "They'll know," the proprietor said. "But I doubt they'll sing into that thing if that's what you're hoping for."

73

John considered the men. An old man had to be dealt with differently than a young one. The former, you had to appeal to his sentimentality, the latter, to his pride. But here they were, all of them together, and he thought it was a shame his Ediphone was such a hard sell with the cowboys. He turned to the proprietor. "If I'm still talking to them in five minutes, bring over a round of whatever they're drinking."

"And for you?"

"What've you got?"

"Best sour mash in the state."

"That's fine."

"If it's Negro songs you want, you best go to the Black Elephant, down on Rusk Street in Hell's Half Acre." John nodded his thanks and made his way over to the table in the corner.

"Hello," he began, trying to hold the machine casually. "I'm from Harvard University, and I'm travelling around the country collecting cowboy songs with my Edison recording device."

The youngest of the men, holding his cards to his chest, said, "You ain't recording me now, are ya?" and John assured him that he wasn't. The man waved John away and looked back at his cards.

The drinks arrived, the proprietor having ignored John's instructions. That broke the awkwardness a bit, and after a long pause the old man asked John to sit.

"Does one of you have a song you want put down?" John asked.

"Everybody knows them songs," said the second young man, who had a deep scar on his lip. "Only a damn fool would spend his time trying to set down songs everybody knows."

John looked at his boots. "You know, I'm a Texan, and I was raised to stick up for my own, which is why I want to make good and sure that Western traditions are treated with the same respect as those of the other regions."

"What part of Texas you from?" asked the one with the scar.

"I grew up in Bosque County. My father's ranch was along a branch of the Chisholm Trail. I remember one night as I was falling asleep, I heard a cowboy singing 'The Old Chisholm Trail', and ever since that day, it's my favourite song. I don't s'pose any of you knows it."

The one with the scar laughed. "Listen, *professor*," he said. "That song is as long as it takes to get from Texas to Montana. I can sing eighty-nine verses myself, some of which would burn up that old horn, but no way am I goin' to poke my face up to that blamed thing and sing. The tune ain't much, no how."

John was about to give up when the old man spoke. "Back in the seventies, we sang it all the way from San Antonio to Dodge City. There never was a day that someone didn't build a new verse."

"Do you remember any of them?"

"'Course I do! How am I gonna forget that?"

"Would you like to sing some of it for me?"

"No," the man said. "I'll tell you something better. I'll tell you a song I wrote myself, with the help of my friends, when we was buffalo hunters."

"All right," said John. "Let me get set up here." He stood, but the man went cold.

"I was gonna tell you, is all," he said, so John left the

machine and sat back down, taking a pencil and paper from his pocket to record the words.

"Right," the man said. "In the summer of '73, me and some others was hired by a man named Crego for the buffalo hunt, me bein' one of two sharpshooters, plus four others to skin, and a camp cook." He looked at each man in turn as he spoke. "He, that's Crego, was the manager, so he was s'posed to sell the skins and give us the money. Now, we got a helluva lot of huntin' done that season, but come the end Crego told us he had lost our money in gambling and couldn't pay us. So we shot old Crego and left his bones to bleach where we had left so many hundreds of stinking buffalo." Here the man stopped and looked at John. "Then we headed back to Jacksboro, and on the way we would shape up this song every night when we camped, and we called it 'The Buffalo Singers.'"

The old man sang his song to John, who tried to write down the words, knowing that the man wouldn't repeat them.

> Oh it's now we've crossed the Peace River and
> homeward we are bound.
>
> No more in that hell-fired country shall we ever be
> found.
>
> Go home to our wives and sweethearts, tell others
> not to go.
>
> For God's forsaken the buffalo range and the damned
> old buffalo.

After that John left, planning to go to The Black Elephant and try his luck there. It also occurred to him, as it always did when he travelled in the South, to ask after Nat. On his way to his vehicle, he saw a blind old man strumming a guitar and singing, so he put down his recording device, put a coin in the man's tin cup, and listened until the song ended.

"What was that you played?" John asked in a slow, loud voice. The man shrugged.

"You don't know the name?"

"I made it up," the man said.

"Right now?"

"Yes."

"Could you sing it again?"

"No."

John clenched his teeth. "Do you know other songs?"

"What kind of songs?"

"Songs that tell stories."

"No," the man said, standing up. "But if you'll walk me home for my lunch, my wife knows all the songs in the world." He groped with his free hand until he found John's arm.

"I have my automobile here, we could…"

"No automobile can go where I live," the man said. "If you're comin' you gotta walk."

The old man led them through the stockyards, over the tracks and down to the lowland around the Trinity River, John balancing his machine on his hip and watching both the old man's steps and his own. Through the trees, John could see a tin-roofed caravan, its stovepipe releasing a thin trail of smoke. Next to the caravan was a bright red tent, and beside it a young woman with long black hair was seated. She wore a red and purple brocade costume, and her hands and ears were laden with silver and gems. The old man kissed this woman on the mouth before disappearing into the tent, leaving John to introduce himself to her. She shook his hand but didn't offer her name.

"I'm told that you know a number of songs."

"I do," she said.

"I'm collecting songs in this machine. To preserve them, you know?" He thought it best not to mention Harvard or his book. The woman smiled.

"You want me to sing into your machine?"

"That would be wonderful."

"Why don't you say so?"

A man came out of the tent, but it was not the same man who had gone in. His hair was black now, his shoulders broad and straight, his glasses removed to reveal clear black eyes. He walked robustly toward John and the woman, smiling at John, who understood with some hint of admiration that the man was an utterly convincing faker.

"So, she gonna sing for ya?" the faker asked.

A tall black man came out of the caravan and wordlessly set about preparing food.

"That your cook?" John asked.

"He cooks," said the faker.

"Does he know any songs?"

"Ask him yourself." He turned. "Bill, the gentleman has a question for you."

John cleared his throat. "I was wondering if you know any songs you might sing for me."

"Sure I do," the man said.

"Will you sing for me?" John asked.

"Sure I will," said the man in a friendly way. "As soon as I'm finished here."

"Okay!" John turned to the woman. "Do you mind if we get started?"

She shook out her hair and sat up straight.

"We'll eat first," the faker said. "Then they can both sing for you."

The cook served them beans and potatoes while the faker explained how he and his wife operated. "We do teamwork here," he said. "We aim to please our customers, and I think we do. My wife shakes down the saps that like to hold her hand while she reads their fortunes, and all the self-righteous fools go away from my tin cup happy, marking down one more good deed on their passports to heaven. Meanwhile, we travel all over."

After they had finished their meal, the faker lay down in the mesquite grass to listen to his wife. John thought they'd had an understanding about her singing into the machine, but when he began to set it up, she wagged her finger at him. He settled on the grass next to the faker and took out his paper and pencil, but she shook her head, so he put them away.

She sang the first blues he had ever heard, which moved him to tears, plus several other songs of the road that were new to him. After a while, he began to feel intoxicated by the luxury of giving those songs up. He thought of Shirley, his first sweetheart, who, when she was sure that she would die before getting home to Texas, wrote out the words to Tennyson's "In Memoriam" and sealed them in a watertight package addressed to him, which she tossed off the ferry in New Jersey.

The woman ended by singing 'Git Along Little Dogies.'

"To me that's the loveliest of the cowboy songs," she said. "You mustn't frighten the cattle. They get nervous and worry when thunder comes. Lope around them gently in the darkness as you sing about punching them along to their new home. They'll sleep through the night and never have a bad dream."

The cook's songs were the old Methodist hymns of John's youth, with the fire and brimstone imagery that had brought on his childhood nightmares about drowning in oceans of blood. Watching the man sing, John began to compose in his mind a letter to his wife, Bess. He would tell her how tender were his feelings for the man, thinking about the hopeless struggle before him and his people. The end of slavery had only widened the gulf that separated white and black, he would tell her, creating more distrust and fear than there had ever been.

When the cook had finished, John thanked him and showed him how the machine worked. "Ever heard of a man named Nat Blythe," he asked before they parted. The man thought it over for a while.

"What's he to you?"

"He was my friend," John said. "He worked on my father's ranch."

"What he look like?"

"I don't remember."

"Might make it hard to find him," the man said.

"When he turned twenty-one, the boss he was indentured

to gave him his savings and sent him on his way. Before he left he took me to town and had two pictures made of me, one for each of us." John pulled out a photograph of himself as a 12-year-old boy. "This is the only thing I have to remember him by."

"He didn't say where he was goin'?" the cook asked.

"His friends said he was murdered for his money, and his body was thrown into the Bosque River."

"I bet that's where he is then."

John shook his head. "He gave my life its bent. He sang all the time."

All the way back to the saloon, John thought about Nat. It was as if Nat's liberty had become real to him for the first time when he saw the chained and ornamented elephant trudging over the plains, and in some fatal confusion of symbols, that image had lingered in his mind as a promise of freedom and possibility. John would never be able to imagine that same person bound with baling wire and weighted down with scrap iron at the bottom of the Bosky. He would never give up hope that somehow, like that poem that Shirley threw into the ocean without any promise of its delivery, Nat would someday be found and sent back home.

1988
Nuclear Heartland

ANGE STARED AT HER FATHER'S HAIRY HANDS on the steering wheel. How gross, she thought. He's like an ape. "Next is Holy Terror," he said. "Read me the instructions."

She opened the guidebook and searched for the name. Her finger traced the pages that were most heavily marked with his messy handwriting, past Contaminated Forevermore and Prairie Primeval until she found it, between To Be or Not to Be and Whamo Grano Blamo.

"It says after we pass the railroad tracks in Greene we should go north two dot five miles on State Highway 28," she read. "Then go right two dot seven miles."

"Point seven," he said. "The dot means point."

"Missile is on the left."

A spear of underwire bit into her left side as she turned to look out the back window at the dust rising between the car and the barbed wire fence surrounding Justice Stops Here. She wished she had the nerve to ask him, so she could think about something else. Maybe she could make a joke about it, like it was no big deal, but if she was going to do that, she should have done it when he mentioned the motel, which was hours ago. If she said something now, it would seem like that was all she'd thought about in the meantime.

"Are these the railroad tracks?" he said, suddenly frantic. "How are you supposed to know if this is Greene? There's nothing here!" As usual, she didn't know the answer, but she turned to look out the front windshield to show solidarity with his latest navigational conundrum.

The trip had begun that morning, when he picked her up from her mother's house in Souris, Manitoba. She hadn't slept much because her breasts were throbbing and she couldn't find a comfortable position on her side or back. She used to sleep on her stomach, her hands folded under her like a little angel, but there was no room for her arms any more.

She'd had to rush through breakfast, because she knew it would take at least half an hour to rig up the beige granny bra from Eaton's that she had converted into a kind of binding device. First, she pulled the bra over her head and shoulders. Next, she leaned forward and slowly stretched the material over her breasts, one at a time. Finally, she had to disperse each breast within the bra, stuffing the sides under her armpits. After that, there was a whole system of fastening and adjusting involving an arsenal of safety pins. In the end, she'd settled for a slightly lopsided look in exchange for a setup that was bearably painful and unlikely to stab her or come undone.

Meanwhile, her mother had spent the morning carefully arranging her hair and makeup to look like she'd rolled out of bed with perfect skin and gently tousled hair, and the two of them had fought over the bathroom like a pair of teenagers. Ange knew her mother's preparations meant she was planning to come outside when her father arrived. It drove her crazy the way her mother performed for men. With some she played at helplessness, saying things like, "It's so good *you* were here. I have *no idea* about these things." With others, usually the ones Ange liked best, she was cold and arrogant for no reason. With Ange's father, it was always the independent woman routine, which left Ange torn between whatever loyalty she still felt for her mother and her need to distance herself from the embarrassing display.

Despite the various acts her mother put on for men, Ange knew that she hated them all equally. "They're only thinking about one thing," she told Ange, who had been shamed into wearing baggy clothes and keeping her t-shirt on in the pool since she was ten. "They only want you for your body," her mother said, but the way Ange saw it, at fourteen years old, her body was completely trashed anyway. Her breasts were rippled with bruise-coloured stretch marks, her ribs were deformed by the constant rubbing and digging of underwire, her shoulders were rutted with grooves from her bra straps and her spine was probably growing crooked because when she stood up straight the other kids said she was flaunting it.

It had been over a year since Ange had seen her father. When he had called to suggest the trip, he'd talked to her mother for at least five minutes before asking for Ange, who was so preoccupied with trying to figure out why he was talking to her mother that she was defenseless when he asked if she would like to take an "environmental awareness" trip to North Dakota.

In the past, he had often involved her in his activism, which was fine when she was a cute kid having her picture taken holding signs she didn't understand. But as she got older, he'd become increasingly critical of what he called her lack of interest in the world, and since they saw each other so infrequently after he moved to Regina, his criticism eventually became the basis of every conversation they had, until he finally seemed to lose interest in her altogether.

"Just for one night," he'd said, and she'd agreed because she felt sorry for him. She regretted her moment of weakness as soon as it dawned on her that one night meant sleeping arrangements would have to be made, and that the making of those arrangements meant that he must have considered the developments that had taken place since the last time she'd spent a night with him, or worse, that he might not have considered them at all. Now here she was with Holy Terror in her immediate future and the motel beyond that, and all she wanted was her bed at home.

"This one's interesting," said her father, who had calmed down since seeing a sign identifying the place as Greene, North Dakota. "The guy from Nukewatch told me that he was here when they planted it, and the farmer who owned the field was so horrified he put his farm up for sale the next day. He thought it was going to be a batch of dynamite or something, not a forty-ton intercontinental ballistic missile!"

Ange pressed her lips together and nodded her head to indicate impressed surprise, but the truth was that measurements like this meant nothing to her. A ton, a kilometre, an acre—she was incapable of conceptualizing such abstractions.

The world, to her, consisted of the known, which had dimensions that could be seen and felt, and the unknown, which did not. Travelling through the prairies with her father, she had no sense of north or south or of what distance they were from Souris, let alone the USSR, a place that occupied a dark corner of her imagination along with various other things that were, due to being so often discussed but never experienced, suspended somewhere between known and unknown, such as World War II and the nucleus of a cell.

Sex had occupied that same strange space in her psyche, casting its glow over all the frightening things that dwelled there, until she'd allowed James Betker to finger her in the back of the school bus and then, two weeks later, let Matthew Cain take her to his dad's hunting camp. "You taste like a peach," Matt had said when they kissed on the dank futon under a lamp in the shape of a miniature guillotine, and although she'd thought it was a stupid thing to say, she had liked it. Feeling suddenly playful, she'd said, "I'm freezing," and moved his hand to her erect nipple, then, when he tried to take off her shirt, she'd jumped off the couch and said, "Let's light the wood stove!" in a voice so foolishly childlike it made her blush.

Hurrying over to the stove, she had felt him pursuing her, but not the way she wanted. When she bent down to open the filthy glass door, he had grabbed her from behind and pressed his erection into her butt cheek, and when she had turned to him looking pained and confused, he'd said, "You'd better be ready to finish what you started." All at once, with a sickening disappointment that felt somehow familiar, she had discovered that she had no choice about what happened to her, and that the promise of power and something like glory sex had once extended to her had proven, like everything else, to be a miserable lie.

When they arrived at Holy Terror it was almost dusk, and the corn hissed like a field of punctured tires. Ange and her father got out of the car and approached the site in silence, her father heading straight for the sign that read, "Warning: Restricted Area." When they got close, they heard the mechanical whirr of the security camera over the hum that came from inside the fence. "Hey," her father said, waving. "We're on Candid Camera." He moved toward her to parody a happy family pose, but she stepped aside and gave both him and the camera a stiff smile as she stared at the concrete slab through the metal links.

The cold wind ruffled her windbreaker and made the fence shake. She could feel her bra coming undone in the back, and she found that she had the same feeling she used to get as a child when she had to call her mother in the middle of the night to pick her up from a sleepover. Some small thing, like bumping into her friend's dad on her way back to bed from the bathroom, left her feeling shamefully exposed, caught in an act that was meant to be private.

He had brought the guidebook with him, and he opened it and showed her the page. "This is what it looks like under there," he said, pointing to a heavily-marked diagram of something that looked not unlike the things she'd seen Wile E. Coyote light with a match in *Road Runner* cartoons. "That thing is forty times more powerful than the bomb that was dropped on Hiroshima. Can you imagine?"

What she had understood so far was that the concrete slab

was a lid, under the lid was one of a thousand missiles that were buried under farmers' fields across the prairies and aimed at the Soviet Union, and because of this they were all sort of doomed. When they'd first set out that morning and her father had begun his lecture, Ange had asked a few questions, such as how do missiles know where they're going without someone driving and what if they hit a bird or a plane on the way, but after a while, she felt so impressed that someone had figured all of this out and so stupid for knowing so little that she decided to sit quietly and try to react appropriately to what her father said without giving away too much. Specifically, she wanted him to think that she cared about the missiles without offering any accompanying indication that she cared about him.

"It could destroy an entire civilization in a second," he said.

She made a concerned face. Of course he wouldn't expect her to sleep in the same bed as him, she thought. There was no way he was that clueless. But even sleeping in the same room would be unbearably awkward and awful.

"And of course the Russians have missiles too. Can you guess where they're aimed?"

She waited to see if he would answer his own question, as he often did. "Where?"

"Think about it."

"I don't know. Washington?" She knew that there was a DC and a state, but she didn't know the difference and thought it was too late to ask.

Her father laughed. "No, they're aimed right where we're standing, and the nuclear fallout would blow directly northeast of here. Do you know what that means?"

"No."

"Think about it." She pretended to think about it until he told her the answer.

"Winnipeg would be wiped out, and we'd all get lethal doses of radioactivity. The Pentagon tries to pretend they're here to protect us, but really they're turning us into a human sacrifice to protect the big cities. Can you believe that?"

"I don't know."

"Well come on," he said. "What do you think?"

She shrugged and wrapped her arms around herself, feeling miserable that the only thing she had to look forward to was an even more unpleasant scenario than the one she was currently enduring.

"I'm interested to know your opinion. Can you tell me your opinion?"

"Well…who has more, them or us?"

"It doesn't matter, Ange. There's no remainder, if that's what you're thinking."

"Okay, so I guess…like, I hope it doesn't happen," she said.

"But doesn't it make you angry?"

"I guess."

"And do you think there's anything you can do about it, or do you want to wait and see what happens?"

"I don't know," she said.

"I guess, I guess, I don't know." He tensed his mouth and moved his head from side to side. "You don't care, do you?"

She said, "I guess not" at the same time as he was saying, "You sound exactly like your mother," then she turned and walked back to the car.

In Mohall they ate pizza in silence, and she used a fork and knife instead of her hands. Afterward, they made the short drive to the motel.

"I'm sorry, okay?" he offered. "There are a lot of things you don't understand yet because I've never been willing to drag you into all that grown up stuff." He was quiet for a moment before continuing. "You know, your mother always cared more about outfits than anything we were trying to accomplish, and it's because of people like her that it all went to shit."

Ange looked out the window at a group of boys picking squashes and putting them in canvas bags slung over their shoulders. She thought about what her mother said once. "Ever since you hit puberty, he turned on you. It was like he didn't trust himself around you." Ange knew it wasn't true and that her mother had said it purely out of spite, but it had planted a seed, and that was all it took.

"What I mean," her father said, "is that it's not your fault."

The outside of the motel was the dreariest thing Ange could imagine. The parking lot was empty apart from an old blue pickup, and there wasn't one person in sight. The radio was on in the truck, and country music blared out of its open door over the sound of an argument in one of the units. Ange decided to follow her father to the office so she could find out what the sleeping situation was before she was confronted with it in the room. As they walked, she tried to make out some of the argument, but all she could hear was a woman screaming, "No! This is bullshit!" again and again.

In the office, there was a ginger cat on the counter, and

Ange stroked its fur while her father spoke to the fat man behind the desk.

"Sign here," the man said. He bent down with a loud groan and reappeared with a set of keys. "You're in number 12. License plate number?"

"Why do you need that?"

"I need it if you want to park outside your unit."

"Do you have paper and pen?" her father asked, clearly annoyed. The man pushed both across the desk and Ange's father left without looking at her.

"He likes you," the man said once Ange's father was gone. "He doesn't let anybody touch him normally." Ange scratched behind the cat's ears and under his chin. "What's your name, honey?" the man asked. Ange could feel him scrutinizing her tits. People thought they had a right to do that. Everyone felt free to comment and stare.

"Ange," she said, pronouncing it the way the kids at school did, not *Ahnj*, as her mother said it.

"You enjoying your holidays with your daddy?" the man asked. Ange moved her hands to the cat's rump, digging her nails in and massaging above his tail. The man leaned forward and his voice became confiding and soft. "He *is* your daddy, isn't he honey?" Suddenly Ange understood what he was getting at, but in an instant her outrage disintegrated against her will into sudden tears, which fell down her cheeks with the fat man watching, so that she had to run out of the office like a fool.

"Hey, where are you going," her father called after her as she walked away from him down the row of numbered doors.

She was furious beyond all reason. She had no patience for

tears. When her father went to live in Regina, her mother had cried for what seemed like years. Ange had felt her mother's crying in her guts. It tugged like a fishhook in her, and she went toward it not out of love but out of fear of being ripped apart. She would find her mother in her bedroom or in the closet or in the basement, and she would kneel next to her and stroke her hair and say, "It's all right. It's okay," until her mother stopped crying or fell asleep.

It took him so long to come to the room that she started to wonder if something had happened to him. She had been sitting on the concrete stoop, swatting at bugs attracted by the fluorescent lights. Her father was silent as he opened the door, but when she followed him inside she could tell that something was wrong. She barely had a chance to notice that there were two double beds in the room before he turned to face her.

"What the hell is wrong with you?" he shouted. "That man thought I was some sort of criminal." His face was red and spit spattered his lips. Part of her wanted to laugh, because she had never seen him so out of control. "Do you have any idea how embarrassing that was for me?" She kept walking toward the bathroom, planning to lock herself in and make a bed of towels in the bath, but as she passed him he grabbed her hard around the fattest part of her arm and spun her around, so they were face to face.

It was the first time he had touched her in years, but it wasn't his roughness that made her feel violated, it was the intimacy of his hand against her bare skin. Feeling an urgent need to reverse what he had done, she leaned forward and bit into the soft flesh of his shoulder. Her teeth almost penetrated the skin before he socked her on the right side of her head and she fell, ears ringing, onto the floor.

When she opened her eyes, her father stood over her, his hand still raised. She was lying on her side, her cheek pressed into the disgusting carpet. He knelt down and she covered her face, expecting him to hit her again. He tried to move her hands. She started to turn on her belly to get up, but he grabbed her around her waist from behind. They struggled on the floor. His arms reached around her on both sides, and he held his right forearm with his left hand over her chest. He wound his ankles around her legs to stop her from kicking him.

Her cheek was stinging and hot, and warm liquid leaked out of her nose and into her hair. An opened safety pin had stabbed her right shoulder, and she could feel it working its way in rhythmically with her sobs. The sound of her own crying infuriated her, but there was nothing she could do to stop it and trying only made it worse, so she gave in and told herself that she was totally ruined. She couldn't stop crying and she couldn't make him let her go, so she lay in his arms and thought about being ruined until he lifted her into the bed and rocked her to sleep.

When she woke up, it was morning. Her face still ached and her head felt heavy. She could hear him in the shower. She tried to sit up, but when she lifted her head she discovered that it was stuck to the stiff orange top quilt, the one that her mother had always told her to remove before sleeping in a hotel bed, because they were never washed. She slowly peeled the quilt away from her face and turned to see that the other bed was still made.

She stood and went over to the wardrobe mirror. One side of her face was bright pink, and there was dried snot caked under her nose. She undid the top two buttons of her shirt and lifted one sleeve over her shoulder to see where the safety pin had stabbed her. The tip had punctured her skin below the shoulder blade, but it was easy to pull out. She refastened it through two loops in the strap of her bra, buttoned her shirt and pushed hard on the place where the pin had been to soak up any blood.

It was weird how okay everything felt, even with the bathroom door about to open and not knowing how her father would behave. She sat on the bed and waited, and when she got bored with waiting she turned on the TV and flipped through the channels.

When her father came out of the bathroom, he was holding a steaming facecloth. He offered it to her, and she pressed it to her cheek. She thought he looked like a little kid who doesn't know what to do, and she felt sorry for him, but the feeling was different than the one that had made her agree to the trip. He watched her dab her face with the facecloth, and then they both silently packed their things and took their bags outside.

"Do you have the guidebook?" he asked as she climbed into the car. She closed her door, opened the glove box and showed him the book. When both of their seatbelts were on, he lifted her hand from her lap and squeezed it in his until it almost hurt. They stayed there for a minute, staring at the grimy white vinyl exterior of the motel, and she could feel his pulse in her fingers.

As they drove home, they passed the squash boys again, and

she waved to them, but they didn't see her. Then there were two fields of wheat, one on either side of the highway. There was more wheat there than she had ever imagined was possible. It went on and on. There must be enough to feed the whole country, she thought. There must be enough, probably, to feed the whole world. And to think that there were people who knew how to harvest it and turn it into flour, and other people who knew how to turn flour into bread. How clever people were, she thought, and how much there was of everything.

1872
Home on the Range

I CAN NAME ONE HUNDRED trees or more. Sycamore, cottonwood, birch, oak, ash, cedar, weeping willow. I don't have to think about it, I just know, as you know the names of your friends and do not have to consider their physical characteristics before deciding what to call them. As always, when I pass the line of trees by the river and am about to come upon my dugout, I anticipate the worst. An Indian raid, perhaps, some murderous wanderer, or a pack of wild dogs eating my vittles. But no, everything is as I left it, and perhaps some part of me is disappointed. This is not what I want. I do not want to go down into that damp room and sit alone with my Bible and my dark thoughts. I want a proper log cabin, and I want back everything I ran away from, but I want it to be different this time, and this time I will be different too.

I give Honey some hay and leave her for the night. Inside I fumble with the lantern until I have enough light. I clear the table, lay out my pen and paper, and, as happens every time,

I sit down to write and don't know how to begin. I think of my mother. When I was in medical school I saw her in a dream. I was lying on the floor and she was looking down at me. I reached out to touch her, and I caught the hem of her dress, but she recoiled. I sat up and took her by the wrist, but she shook me off. She went away without saying a word. I woke myself up with weeping. I tried to record it in a poem, but it fell so miserably short of expressing what I felt, I was left with only a sickening emptiness.

I suppose I am compelled to think these pathetic thoughts because they help stimulate a frame of mind that is conducive to truth. I need these feelings in order to perceive the connections between the past and the present, the individual and the universal, but it is so difficult for me. I am always striving, never coming near my goal. I conjure my mother's face, an amalgam of all the women I have known. I conjure them because I want to feel the sublime pain of my longing and to be moved to put down those lines that have been turning over in my mind for days. I hold them there—the women and the lines and the longing—as I begin to write.

1947
Here In The Grass We Will Lie

INEZ HAD HER HANDS IN THE DOUGH.

"Bruce," she shouted. "There's someone at the door." The radio was on in the living room. She poked her head through the doorway, her hands held up, sticky with wet flour. She could see her son's bare feet waving in the air, but he didn't answer her. "Bruce," she said again. He still didn't respond. "For goodness sakes," she shouted. "Harry, someone's at the door."

"I'm shaving," came the response from the laundry room.

Inez quickly rubbed the dough off her hands. She looked in the hall mirror and saw that she still had her curlers in. She pulled them out as quickly as she could, but it was too late, the knocking had stopped.

Now someone was tapping on the back door. From that vantage point, whoever it was would be able to see Harry in the laundry room. Yes, Harry had answered the knock. She could hear him talking to another man. She hoped he had wiped the shaving cream from his face and put on a clean shirt.

"Inez," he called, finally. "This is Homer Croy. He's here to talk about grandfather's poetry." She flattened her hands along the fabric of her apron and went out into the entranceway, where a man with a long, pale face and sparse white hair stood next to her husband.

"Pleased to meet you, Mr. Croy," she said.

"And you," he said. She shook his hand, and there was an awkward silence.

"Come and sit down," Harry said, taking Mr. Croy by the arm and leading him into the living room. "I expect you'd like to talk to my father."

There was another silence before Mr. Croy said, "You mean...is he...I didn't realize any of his sons were still alive."

"He's upstairs," said Harry. "Let me get him."

Harry came into the kitchen, speaking to Inez in a forced whisper as he hurriedly grabbed a necktie from the ironing board. "Go and get Father," he said. "The man wants to talk to him." Inez rolled her eyes. "And why haven't you offered him something to drink?"

"What does he want?" she asked.

"He's writing about my grandfather. He wants to talk to someone who knew him."

"Well, he's come to the wrong place," Inez said. Harry frowned.

"Go and get Father, dear."

"He's taking a nap."

"Wake him up. Bring him a cup of tea."

As she went upstairs to wake her father-in-law, she heard her husband taking down boxes from the top shelf in the hall cupboard. "I have his letters here as well," Harry called to Mr. Croy, and Inez felt angry with him for being willing to put everything on display for a stranger.

Bruce Sr. was lying awake in bed with the sheets held up to his chin, as if he were peering out over a wall. He looked at Inez warily.

"Can I help you?" he said.

"Harry would like you to come down and meet someone, Father."

"What's that?" he asked, cupping his hand to his ear.

"There's a man who wants to talk to you about your father."

"I'll have to come and speak with him, I suppose," he said. He rose slowly and shifted his legs over the side of the bed. Once he was there, he looked at her as if wondering how he had done it before, until she began to dress him.

The coffee table was covered with poems and letters written by the stranger Harry had so often bragged about. Mr. Croy was reading aloud a poem her husband's grandfather had written, called "A Dream in Which I Saw My Mother." Inez felt embarrassed for her family and angry with the man for coming there and reading that poem like he was, rolling the Rs and pronouncing every syllable as if it were a masterpiece.

"Did any of the other members of your family write poetry?" Mr. Croy asked Harry.

"No. Not one," Harry said. "Except for my wife. She writes some poems. Don't you, dear?"

From the creak of the stairs Inez knew Bruce Sr. had begun his laboured descent. Mr. Croy stood up and stayed standing for the full five minutes it took for the old man to get downstairs and into the living room, where he caught his breath while gripping the back of a chair.

"You say it's a man to see me?" he said, peering dimly around the room.

"Yes, Father," said Harry.

"Would he be wantin' to put some questions?"

"Yes, Father. He's a writer."

The old man seemed more pleased than Inez had seen him in months. "Would they be about my racehorses?" he asked.

"No, he wants to ask about your father."

"Oh, well, what has he got in mind?"

Mr. Croy leaned forward and waited while Inez helped Bruce Sr. into his chair. "Did your father ever talk about his writing?" he asked once Bruce was in his seat.

"Oh, he was always writin' off poetry. I didn't think much of it. He was a good parent to me. Never laid a hand on me in his life." Inez thought that this wasn't saying much, since Bruce had barely known his father; she felt sad and thought about her own father, who she hadn't known, not because he wasn't present but because he was unknowable.

"Harry, shall I tell him about Alice Coffman?" Bruce Sr. asked.

"No. He wants to hear about your father's poetry."

"Oh, I don't mind," said Mr. Croy. Inez excused herself and went back into the kitchen to listen to the familiar tale from a distance as she put her father-in-law's dinner on a plate.

"Alice Coffman was the best horse I ever trained. She was known around Little Rock, Arkansas, as 'The Horse that Wouldn't Start,' but she would start for me!" Inez thought how good it was that he only loved his story more now that he was unaware he had told it a thousand times, changing it slightly with each telling.

"Yes, I started in to train Alice Coffman and pretty soon I got her so she would go. It was by tryin' to understand her, you see? It takes quite a bit to understand a horse." He paused. Inez could hear the sounds of gunfire and galloping horses on her son's radio program. She wondered if her father-in-law was crying, as he often did when he got talking about his horses, but he soon continued with his story.

"When I spoke the word, she was off. I've trained a good many horses, but I never had one I thought as much of as I did Alice Coffman. Would you like to hear about the time they telegraphed New York because they believed she was a ringer?"

"He wants to know about your father," Harry said.

"There ain't much to be said. One of his poems became favourably known. He used to play the fiddle; we liked that."

"And did you ever visit the cabin where he composed his poetry?" asked Mr. Croy.

"I suppose you've heard of Jesse James," Bruce Sr. said. "Well, his brother Frank James used to work with me in Arkansas. If Alice Coffman had been a ringer, I would have gone to the pen. But I never engaged in anything of a questionable nature. I tell you she was a good horse and you've got to believe me."

Inez came back into the living room and saw Mr. Croy with his hand on Bruce Sr.'s shoulder. Her husband was shuffling some papers around on the coffee table.

"I've got your dinner ready, Father," she said.

He looked at her lovingly. To Mr. Croy he said, "I'm

thankful I've still got my appetite. I've got lots of things to be thankful for. My son makes me a good home and Ruby is good to me. Did I give you what you wanted about Alice Coffman?"

"You did, Mr. Higley."

The old man rose slowly, took three steps toward the kitchen, turned around again and said, "It took three weeks to learn her to start!" before taking Inez's arm and letting her help him to his place at the table.

"I'm not Ruby, Father," Inez said as she opened a paper napkin and draped it across his lap.

"Oh," he said. "Ruby was a good girl."

"I'm sure she was, but I'm not her. I'm Inez."

"I know," he said.

Inez could hear her husband telling Mr. Croy his own tired story about the one time he met his grandfather, an experience he only remembered remembering. "I was born in 1905," Harry said, "so I must have been seven years old then, but I'll never forget it. He told me that a great war was coming, and the sky would be filled with airships and the roads would be crowded with vehicles."

"Incredible," Mr. Croy said.

As she carefully combined peas, beet cubes and triangles of steak on Bruce Sr.'s fork, Inez listened to Harry tell Mr. Croy about how *Life Magazine* had come to interview them several years back, and how Admiral Richard E. Byrd had so loved the song version of his grandfather's poem, he'd taken the record with him when he was stationed alone at the South Pole.

She was feeding Bruce Sr. his ice cream when Harry called into the kitchen to say that he and Mr. Croy were going to see his grandfather's grave. Mr. Croy asked Inez if she would like to join them, and she decided she would, because it was still a beautiful day. She wondered if Harry would pretend that he'd been there before. The truth was that none of them had been, except Bruce Sr., who went once on his own at least twenty years earlier. His brother's widow had asked him to read the epitaph from "An Elegy Written in a Country Churchyard" at the funeral, but he had refused, saying that he wouldn't feel honest about it.

Inez found herself thinking again about her own father, and whether she would visit his grave someday with her son to carry on this business of memorializing people they had never known, as if something a person had scribbled or the place his bones would be buried should mean more once he was dead, and she should forget that he wouldn't have given an Indian nickel for her when he was alive.

Bruce Jr. didn't look up when Inez brought Bruce Sr. into the living room and sat him on the couch with a blanket on his lap. "Take care of your grandfather," she said. "We'll be back shortly." Her son didn't respond.

"Bruce," she said again.

"It's time for The Triple B Ranch, Mother," he said without looking at her. She smiled and thought how she loved him, little radio worshipper, and Harry too.

She put on her coat and hat and followed her husband and Mr. Croy out of the warm house into the cool fall afternoon. She stopped to observe the progress of a sluggish wasp dragging its way across the front steps, and she wondered if she should shut a couple of windows against the cooling air, but decided against it. As she closed the door, from inside she could hear the sound of Buffalo Bob greeting his radio audience with a cheerful *Oh, ho, ho, howdy doody*.

1935
Report of Samuel Moanfeldt,
on his Investigation

I SHOULD BEGIN BY acknowledging that I have already written a report of my investigation. If you have read that report, much of this will be repetition. However, it is not the same report. I could not have written this report then, and I could not write that report now. Then I was young and sharp, now I am old and sentimental. Then I had the facts, now I have the feelings. I had the feelings then too, but I wasn't able to express them, and in any case no one asked.

The objectives of my investigation, as stated in my initial report to the Music Publishers Protective Association, were to establish the following:

    1. That the song "Home on the Range" was in the public domain by reason of the fact that it had been known and sung generally throughout the country in 1885 or prior thereto

2. The author and composer of the words and tune of this song, if possible

3. To find, if possible, some printed record, whether same be an original document, newspaper article or any book or songbook, in which the song is mentioned, or in which the words of the song or music thereof are contained

The unstated objective of my investigation was to expose Mr. and Mrs. William Goodwin of Tempe, Arizona, as a pair of feckless cheats and liars. In 1934, the Goodwins claimed authorship of the song they called "Arizona Home," saying they had written it together and copyrighted it in 1905. Now, the latter part of their claim was true, but that was only proof of their shameless dishonesty. It was my job to prove that the song was in the public domain so that the Goodwins would have to drop their outrageous (to the tune of $500,000) lawsuit, one that barely stopped short of implicating anyone who had ever dared hum the tune.

I had never heard of "Home on the Range" before I was approached to investigate its origins. I first heard of it in a meeting with Phil Dickson of the MPPA in which he asked if I would be interested in taking "The Home on the Range Case." I bluffed a bit, and when he mentioned that it would involve travel, I immediately said that I would take it. I'd never been more than a few miles west of the Hudson in those days, and I was anxious to see first-hand how people lived out west, to get a better sense of the country I had travelled half way across the globe to fight for.

When I admitted to Phil that I had no idea what "Home on the Range" was, he stared at me, waiting to see if I were joking. "It's the most popular song in America, Sam," he said.

I didn't know how to respond, because in those days I didn't listen to music much, apart from my wife Goldie's opera records, which she had inherited from her mother.

When I began my investigation, Goldie was pregnant. She had been quite desperately blue since the beginning of her pregnancy, and I was worried about leaving her, but also, I have to admit it, the idea of having a break from her appealed to me. We argued a great deal in the weeks leading up to my departure. On the day I left, she took a Thermos from the refrigerator to fill with hot coffee for me, and the glass inside bust when she poured the coffee in. Then came the waterworks.

I had no idea how long I would be gone, or even where I would be going. I guessed it would take about a month, but I told her to be prepared for longer, since I had no concrete plan and would have to go wherever the evidence took me. We sat in silence throughout breakfast, but when it was time for me to leave she came around and gave me a kiss at the door. I told her that I hoped she would be herself again when I got back, which was insensitive of me, but I didn't know it at the time.

The first stop on my journey was to be at the home of a Professor Jordan in Columbia, Missouri. A woman named Mrs. Giddeon had written to the MPPA to say that she remembered singing "Home on the Range" at the Stanberry Normal School in 1880, when she was a student there. Professor Jordan was one of several classmates she named who could back up her claim, and being a professor, his statement would carry weight. I had written to tell him I was coming but had not heard back, so I was set to travel all the way from New York to Missouri with no reason to believe I would even find the man I was looking for.

Whenever I am alone on trips, I like to sing to myself. I don't think this is an unusual pastime. From my home to Professor Jordan's home, I sang almost constantly, until I was hoarse. I believe I mostly sang songs from the *Threepenny Opera*, which Goldie and I had seen off-Broadway before it was popular.

Between New York and Missouri I was pleasantly surprised by the cleanliness and general neatness of the motor courts where I stayed and the small restaurants and diners where I ate my simple meals. In Illinois I stopped at a Steak'n'Shake and spent an hour and a half composing my first postcard to Goldie, trying to keep my tone cheerful without letting her think that I was having too wonderful a time without her. I left that diner to find that someone had siphoned most of the gas out of my Buick—a nuisance more than anything, since a gas station wasn't far off.

Professor Jordan was out when I arrived, but through a series of inquiries I was directed to two women who had also been students at Stanberry Normal School. I interviewed them both, and both swore they had sung "Home on the Range" in school assemblies and other student gatherings prior to 1890. One of the ladies, Mrs. Mable White, insisted on singing the song a cappella, and I found it strangely stirring in its simplicity. Afterward, as an aside, I asked Mrs. White if she had any idea who had written it, and she suggested that no one had, that it was a song of the people and should remain so. I include here the words, for those unfamiliar with them:

Oh, give me a home where the buffalo roam,
Where the deer and the antelope play,
Where seldom is heard a discouraging word
And the skies are not cloudy all day.

Home, home on the range,
Where the deer and the antelope play,
Where seldom is heard a discouraging word
And the skies are not cloudy all day.

Where the air is so pure, the zephyrs so free,
The breezes so balmy and light,
That I would not exchange my home on the range
For all of the cities so bright.

The red man was pressed from this part of the West,
He's likely no more to return,
To the banks of Red River where seldom if ever
Their flickering campfires burn.

How often at night when the heavens are bright
With the light from the glittering stars
Have I stood here amazed and asked as I gazed
If their glory exceeds that of ours.

Oh, I love these wild flowers in this dear land of ours,
The curlew I love to hear scream,
And I love the white rocks and the antelope flocks

That graze on the mountain-tops green.

Oh, give me a land where the bright diamond sand
Flows leisurely down the stream;
Where the graceful white swan goes gliding along
Like a maid in a heavenly dream.

I spent the next morning poking around Columbia, talking
about the song with shopkeepers and gas station attendants.
All of them were friendly, and most of them knew the song,
but no one could remember how they knew it, or for how
long they had known it. One young man said that since it was
a cowboy song I should go to Dodge City, as there were still
plenty of people who could remember that place in its heyday.
I kept from him my utter ignorance of the notion that the song
was a cowboy tune.

When I was on the road again, I found myself looking
forward to having the chance to see in person places that
had been the hubs of gun-slinging cowboy capers in the
pulps and penny dreadfuls of my boyhood. As I drove, the
dust intensified, and after a while the effort it took to breathe
started to drive me berserk. Eventually I was forced to hold
a wet handkerchief over my mouth, even with the windows
up. When I removed the handkerchief to wet it again, it was
caked with red dirt. Eventually I had to open my window a
crack to keep from suffocating in the heat, and when I did that
the Buick filled with that blasted dust, which got into my nose
and eyes and even between my teeth.

The landscape bottomed out as I drove through poor old
Kansas. A withering dryness that made me want to weep

for the people who lived there. And all along there was the persistence of dust on the horizon, and a sky that was cloudless and dark even at midday.

Near Wichita I stopped at a stand selling tobacco and cheap souvenirs and bought Goldie a figure of a buffalo carved out of a piece of petrified wood from Arizona. An Indian woman was selling them, and it's funny what you remember, but I think her name was Angeline. I talked to her for a while about the jewellery and other trinkets she made from the wood, which she said came from ancient trees that had fallen into rivers and hardened there until they were stone. Over the years, the wood grew gems, so that when you cracked it open you never knew what you would find. Goldie's buffalo had a stand under his feet with some of those gems on it, and his body had been polished to a sheen. It only cost me twenty-five cents, and I figured Goldie would like it, since she often developed attachments to strange things you wouldn't expect.

When I got to Dodge, I drove around for a while, and I was a bit disappointed. I don't know what I expected— I didn't think there would be gunfighters on every corner and dance hall girls doing the cancan down Front Street—but I hadn't anticipated a quiet, respectable-looking town with a young man dressed in a parody of cowboy garb sitting on a bench in front of the bank sucking on a lollipop.

At the offices of the *Dodge City Globe*, I met Erasmus Adams, editor of the paper and the town's postmaster. I told Adams about my investigation, and he listened with the most sincere attention, interrupting only occasionally to ask a question. I asked him if he would be willing to write an article about my search. He said he would be only too happy to play a small part in the important work I was doing, and he hoped I would get to the bottom of it right there in Dodge. I told him that it was not my goal to discover who had written the song, only to prove that it was known prior to 1885, but he was focused on trying to find the correct adjective to put before my name and title in the article he was already beginning to compose. I told him I had better be going, because I wanted to check into my hotel, but he insisted on giving me a tour of the town first.

Adams walked me around for a while, pointing out the modern homes, the handsome school and church buildings, the Old Western Hotel and the new Harvey Hotel, the First National Bank and the Santa Fe Station with its large sculpture of two longhorn steer bearing the inscription *My trails become your highways*. The statue that marked the entrance to the cemetery—a cowboy with a six-shooter pistol—bore another inscription, for Dodge was fond of its inscriptions. *On the ashes of my campfire, this city is built.*

That cemetery has turned me off such places forever after. Each grave had some gaudy decoration on it, some had boots sticking out of them, some were partially opened to reveal a backbone or a pelvis. One was entirely open, a sad skeleton huddled in its shallow cavity. Some had humorous epitaphs, such as *Here's the bones of Hirram Burr, who mistook a he-cow for a her*. Next to that was a dead tree with a noose hung from its branch bearing a sign that read *Horse thief Pete was hung on this tree in 1873*.

Adams made some jokes of his own, and I guess he could tell that I was annoyed, because he asked if I thought it was in bad taste. I said I found it strange that folk would make light of how hard a place their town had been, and he argued that the West had a right to be proud of its history. If people were so goody-goody that they were offended by that history, he said, they should go somewhere else.

I asked him if it wasn't a sin to desecrate graves like this, but he assured me that the graves were fake and the real bodies had been removed decades earlier. After that he offered to take me out to see the wagon ruts on the Santa Fe Trail, which the Chamber of Commerce had fought to preserve, but I told him I felt tired and wanted to lie down. He promised to have the article in the paper the next day and, if I would keep him updated on my whereabouts, to forward to me any correspondence resulting from it.

The following day the front-page feature in the *Globe* included the details of the Goodwins' suit and of my investigation, written in ridiculously ripe prose and asking people with any information regarding the song to contact Adams. As luck would have it, this story was picked up by almost every newspaper in the country through the Associated Press, and within a week I found myself in the opposite predicament I'd been in back in Missouri—sorting through hundreds of leads in search of one good one.

I met and procured statements from ex buffalo hunters, ex cowboys, ex coach drivers and others who knew and loved the song. Many of the people I spoke with found a way to work into their testimonies their own famous stories of the past; how they had known Bat Masterson or how Wyatt Earp had stayed in their great uncle's hotel. Others were reluctant to speak about the past and suspicious of every question I asked them. But everyone I spoke to had heard of the song and agreed that it had been generally known among people travelling through that part of the country prior to 1890, and that the music and lyrics were similar or identical, depending on who you asked, to those they had heard on the radio. One woman wrote out fully ten verses by hand, verses decidedly different from those sung to me by Mrs. White in Missouri. These verses spoke of gold mining and the Rio Grande. I think that was the first time I realized what a tangled-up mess the whole thing was.

The number of statements I collected in Dodge City would most likely have been sufficient to win the case against the Goodwins, but based on the flood of letters and telegrams that I received after the appearance of that article in the *Globe*, I decided that I had a responsibility to get to the bottom of the thing rather than simply proving to the court's satisfaction that the Goodwins had not written our country's most beloved song.

People from Maine to Washington wrote the most heartfelt things about how their fathers or mothers or grandfathers had written it, or how they remembered being sung to sleep at night to the images of the swan and the antelope. Others confided that they had penned such-and-such a verse, inspired by incidents they described in perfect detail. It was of course impossible that they were all truthful. Some sent old newspaper clippings or copies of diaries written by their deceased relatives. A woman from Oklahoma wrote that she had penned the verse about the Red Man. The son of a former cowhand told me that his father had thought it sounded better as "I would not exchange my home on the range for all of the cities so bright," so he had changed it around, unwittingly giving the song its name.

You can imagine how such an influx of contradictory evidence, such an overwhelming display of feeling from every corner of the country, might have inspired me to continue my search. What's more, I own that I was not ready to go home. Goldie had agreed to three months, and I didn't want to go back any sooner. She wrote while I was in Dodge, telling me she had read the story in the paper. She seemed strange but not unhappy in the letter; she said she wanted to learn to pray. That unnerved me, so I wrote back to say I loved her and missed her and wouldn't leave her again.

By far the most convincing letter I received as a result of the article was from an executive named Kenneth Clarke, from Paul Pioneer Music Corp. back in New York City. In his letter he stated that the song was originally called "Colorado Home," and that it had been written by a man named Bob Swartz, who had worked as a prospector near Leadville, Colorado. Clarke enclosed the frontispiece from the sheet music published by Paul Pioneer, which included a picture of Swartz, a photostatic copy of a sworn affidavit from Swartz's sister, Laura, and a copy of the original lyrics and music set down in a letter from her brother to her parents in 1885. I will include here the letter, which Swartz wrote from the cabin he called Junk Lane Hotel, where he and his friends used to gather to play music after a long day's work.

Junk Lane, Sunday Feb. 15 '85

Dear Folks,

Well we have originated a new song, music and all, and it's creating quite a stir among the boys all around. It's a farewell waltz, gotten up for the separation of the gang. I have two parts now and want four, and all are enclosed. I got up the tune and Bill most of the words, but we all had a hand in it, as the cabin was full that night and everybody helped make it up. If it keeps on going, it will become a popular western song. As I have nothing else to say, we'll fill this up with the song, and also write the music the best I can for Laura to work out when she gets time. It's waltz time in the key of G.

"COLORADO HOME"

Oh! Give me a home, where the buffalo roam,
And the deer and the antelope play.
Where seldom is heard a discouraging word
And the sky is not cloudy all day.

A Home! A Home!
Where the deer and the antelope play
Where seldom is heard a discouraging word
And the sky is not cloudy all day.

Oh! Give me the hill, and the ring of the drill
In the rich silver ore in the ground

And give me the gulch, where the miners can sluice
And the bright yellow gold can be found.

Oh! Give me the gleam, of the swift mountain stream
And the place where no Hurricanes blow
And give me the Park with the prairie dog bark,
And the mountains all covered with snow.

Oh! Give me the mines, where the prospector finds
The gold in its own native land.
With the hot springs below, where the sick people go
And camp on the banks of the Grand.

Oh! Show me the camp, where the prospectors tramp
And business is always alive.
Where dance halls come first, and faro banks burst,
And every saloon is a dive.

Oh! Give me my steed, and the gun that I need
To shoot game for my own cabin home;
And give me the light of the campfire at night
And the wild Rocky Mountains to roam.

The next day I left for Leadville, Colorado. The most significant memory that I have of that trip is of my drive through
the mountains, during which I more than once thought
I was going to meet my Maker. At times I could hardly hear
or breathe because of the altitude, and sickness, fear, dizziness
and sheer frustration almost drove me to tears, but in the end
I made it, and there was a sense of accomplishment in that for

a city boy like me.

When I arrived in Leadville, I went directly to the office of the local newspaper, the *Herald Democrat*. I showed the editor the picture of Bob Swartz that Clarke had sent me and asked if he recognized Swartz or the names of any of the other men listed as co-writers of the song, for it seemed a gang of them, all gold mining partners, had got up the song together one night. The editor did not know Swartz, but he said he was a personal friend of one of the other authors listed there, a Bingham Graves, and that Graves's daughters lived in the nearby town of Orro. He gave me the address of one daughter, name of Dorothy Bennett, and I left right away.

When I arrived at Dorothy's house, she was out front watering her flowers. I'll never forget it, because I remember thinking how lovely she looked in the sunlight, all dishevelled from hard work. She was about forty, and such a good-looking woman, though not beautiful by any standard. When she heard my car coming down the drive, she turned, and for the first time I saw that frown, that crease of her forehead, which I came to know so well, since she became a dear friend of mine and remains one to this day.

Dorothy was a widow, her husband having died of pneumonia several years earlier. Since that time she had turned her home into a sort of boarding house, which she ran with the help of her eldest son. She had heard about the case, but she didn't understand why it had taken me so long to discover that Colorado was home of the Home, since it had been common knowledge there for decades. I told her the truth, which was that I had been largely ignorant of the song's history when I left New York and hadn't done much research before leaving, preferring to head out and see what there was to be found.

She asked if I were married, and I told her I was. She gave me a wry look then and asked was I happily married, and I was taken aback by her frankness. I did something then that I still can't believe, because it was so unlike me—I told her about Goldie's terrible, incurable unhappiness and how heavy our home seemed, how much heavier it had become the further I was from it. I told her I was afraid to be a father with Goldie as my wife, me looking after two children instead of one. She listened patiently and I felt she understood me and didn't judge me. I had never confided my story to another soul, and that afternoon in her kitchen I felt a burden lift from me as I told her about my life. When I had finished speaking, she said nothing except would I like some soup, and while I ate we talked about the song, as if our earlier conversation had never happened.

Dorothy said that when she was a child her father often sang "Colorado Home" to her and her siblings, and she could remember all the words as he had sung them. She told me a bit about her father, too, what a kind man he had been, and she showed me a photograph of him with Bob Swartz in the California Gulch, where they had mined together. She said her father had spoken of Swartz often, although she had never met him herself, and in recent years she had been in contact with Swartz's sister, Laura, who lived in Pennsylvania.

I showed her the 1885 letter, which she read with interest, as if she hadn't seen it before, and afterward she told me a story about how important a role that letter, in its original, had played in Bob and Laura Swartz's lives. Bob worked at a tavern in Pennsylvania in his final years, and he was fond of telling people he had written the song that the president liked so much and that John Charles Thomas and Lawrence Tibbett were singing on the radio. Of course no one believed him until his sister dug up the original letter he had written her in 1885. He showed the letter to his colleagues, and after that he became known locally as the man who had written the famous song. He died shortly thereafter, and Dorothy said she knew that Laura was glad it had been sorted out by then, and he was assured that his legacy was intact before he passed away.

I stayed in Dorothy's boarding house for two weeks. Every morning we took a long walk, and she came with me sometimes on my errands, which were mostly invented by me in order that I should remain longer in her company. Together we sorted through death notices until we found those belonging to her father and Jim Fouts, another of the Junk Lane boys. She was the one who helped me solve the riddle of the Grand River, which appears in the lyrics and has been mistakenly taken for the Rio Grande. Through her clever detective work we found some old maps that provided proof that the upper part of the Colorado River was known as the Grand River before its name was officially changed in 1925. She also took me to the Glenwood Springs, which are no doubt the "hot springs" in the lyrics of the song. She introduced me to old timers who confirmed that buffalo and antelope were common in the county in her father's youth. In the evenings we ate together outdoors and then stayed up late talking about everything under the sun. I had already written to my employer in

New York, and I was proud of the quick work I had made of the case, quietly congratulating myself every time new evidence was found.

After those two weeks with Dorothy, I received a package from the editor of the newspaper back in Dodge City that changed everything. In the first place, there was a frantic letter from Goldie, who had written to the newspaper not knowing how else to reach me since I hadn't contacted her since I had been in Colorado. She said she couldn't cope and was afraid something awful might happen if I didn't come home soon. The rest of the package was a pile of letters from more people who claimed that their father or brother or uncle had written the song, and at first I thought how good it was that I had found out the truth of the matter once and for all.

I looked through the letters out of vague curiosity, only because Dot was out that day. Skimming through, I found an envelope that held a copy of an article from a small Kansas paper called the *Smith County Pioneer*, which referred to a poem entitled "Oh Give Me a Home Where the Buffalo Roam," published in the same newspaper in 1873. The text of the poem, whose title was later changed by the author to "My Western Home," was included, and apart from omitting the verse about the Red Man, the words were strikingly similar to those I remembered Mrs. White singing to me in Missouri, with none of the gold mining references of the "Colorado Home." In the same envelope was a letter from someone at the Kansas State Historical Society telling me that around the time that the Goodwins' lawsuit was filed, many of the newspapers' records mysteriously disappeared, and there were no known copies of the original 1873 issue. The writer hoped

I would come to Kansas and see for myself how well the people in Smith Center knew this poem and remembered its author, a solitary saddlebag physician named Brewster Higley.

Can you imagine my disappointment? To have thought the matter sorted out, only to discover that my efforts might have been a great waste of time. To have believed in the story of Graves and McCabe and Swartz only to discover that it might have been an elaborate lie that they had for some reason told to their children and grandchildren. I had two choices—I could go home and stick with the Colorado story, or I could go to Kansas and see what the people there had to say. I felt as if I were betraying Dorothy by even considering the possibility of Kansas, but I also felt a renewed sense of responsibility and even curiosity to find out the truth, whatever it was.

By that point Dorothy had begun to insist that I go home to my wife. When I told her I was leaving she said she was glad, and I let her believe I was going straight home to New York. Instead, I went directly to Smith Center, Kansas.

During my drive to Smith Center I encountered my first dust blow, and then I finally knew what people were talking about when they said that it was devastation in Kansas. It began immediately after I had crossed the state line, as if God had organized some special conspiracy against the place.

It was like something out of the Bible. I looked in my mirror to see a strange blurring of the horizon behind me. My first thought was that there was something wrong with the mirror, so I turned to look over my shoulder, and I was horrified to see a wall of dust pursuing me. I tried to speed up, thinking that I could outpace the thing, but as it advanced, it seemed to gain in both size and speed, as if it were sucking the sky into itself. In terror I stopped my car, rolled up my window and prayed. I sat through the storm like that, praying out loud. I couldn't hear a word I said for the strength of the gale against the car. Sand battered my windows with such force I was afraid they would shatter. After half an hour or so, it was over and I could breathe again. I was never so conscious of how good it is to breathe!

When I arrived in Smith Center, I followed my own tradition by going straight to the newspaper offices, here the *Smith County Pioneer*, where the editor greeted me with all possible warmth. He showed me the same 1914 article that I had been sent in Colorado, although this copy was complete and included a letter from the then-editor of the *Pioneer*, stating that he had personally known Higley, who he said had written the song as a poem and then had it set to music by his friend Dan Kelley. I had the editor sign some papers, an exercise that now seemed pointless to me, since almost everyone I met seemed happy to sign documents without a shred of proof that their story was true. I told him about the "Colorado Home," and he smiled and said something to the effect of, "I can understand why they'd want it for their own." I asked him if there was anyone living in the area who had personally known the doctor, and he sent me to the house of a man named Trube Reese, one of the oldest pioneers in the county.

Mr. Reese lived with his eldest daughter, who cared for him, and he was happy to answer my questions about Higley. They had become friends after meeting in 1872 at an indignation meeting against the Indians. He had helped the doctor build his dugout on the banks of Beaver Creek to repay him for removing his gallbladder. He told me a bit about the doctor's life and the hardships he had lived through, and it seems that the poor fellow had good reason to want to live in a place where he wouldn't have to hear discouraging words; it sounds like he had his earful of them in Indiana, where he came from.

Reese told me the story of how a friend of his had been shot in the foot, and he had taken the friend to the doctor's claim and asked the doctor to fix him up, which he did. Afterward, as they sat together quietly, the doctor brought out a poem he kept on a scrap of paper inside his Greek Bible and read it to Reese and his friend. The two liked the poem so much they strongly encouraged him to put it to music, which he did with the help of local-miller-and-sometime-musician Dan Kelley. After that, it was sung at almost every social gathering in the area. I asked if Kelley was still living, and Mr. Reese told me that he was not, but that his brother-in-law, Cal Harlan, lived not far from Reese and would be more than happy to speak with me about the song, which he was one of the first to sing.

I went to the home of Cal Harlan, who was then eighty-six years old, and he gave me the most beautiful rendition of the song, which I recorded on a phonograph record for posterity. I had with me the copy of the poem as it appeared in the *Pioneer* in 1914, and although Harlan was blind, singing only from memory, he didn't miss a word. That was what convinced me: Harlan's singing. It was the most plain, honest thing. I asked him how he felt about the song, and he said he liked it very much, and that it was part of him in a way.

I collected affidavits from the Harlan family and many other residents of Smith County, who all corroborated the story told to me by Trube Reese. One man, named A.E. Daniels, told me that as a boy he had been a distant neighbour of Higley's, and he remembered how strange the man was. He told me that late one afternoon the doctor had decided to get a deer, so he took his gun and went to sit on a tree trunk by the creek to wait for one. When no deer came, he took a piece of paper out of his pocket and began to write down words that were bubbling in his mind. There on that tree trunk, according to Mr. Daniels, the famous song was composed. I enjoyed the story, so I didn't ask him how he could know what the doctor had done when he was sitting alone on his remote claim. I learned that the original copy of the poem had burned along with the rest of Higley's possessions when his wagon caught fire while he was moving to Arkansas, and it struck me as a funny thing that the man who had written so famously about the glories of one place should pull stakes for another.

I asked Daniels to take me to the spot where the song had been written, so I could see for myself the landscape that had inspired the old doctor. The house is near a place called Athol, and we arrived at sunset. Pete Rust, the man renting the property, was out fixing his reel mower. A wagon filled with coal was parked in the driveway. My immediate impression was that there was nothing growing there, so why bother with the mower. The scorched grass crackled under my feet. I began by telling Rust why I was there and asking some general questions about the land, which seemed too hopelessly dry to grow anything. He offered to show us Dr. Higley's log cabin, and as we followed him to the shabby structure I saw for the first time the creek the doctor sat near to write, which is dried up now. As we neared the cabin, I heard a terrible din from inside, and when Rust opened the door, out flew three hens, which he and Daniels caught and put back in.

Can you believe that the site is now used as a henhouse? I asked Rust whether he knew what had taken place there, and he said he knew a pioneer doctor had written a poem. I asked if he didn't think he should keep it proper for sentimental reasons. He shook his head and said he was too short of hen space.

"But don't you ever think about the historic nature of the event that took place here?" I asked.

"Yes, I do sometimes," he said. "On the other hand, I've got used to the idea. An' there's always the hen-space problem. I have to think of that. Sometimes visitors leave gates open. I've got to think of that, too."

I went back to the Harlans' house and passed the evening talking to them about Brewster Higley and Dan Kelley and the days of their youth, and I felt embarrassed to realize how little I understood of other people's lives. They told me about the dust, and how they coped by putting wet gunny sacks in the windows and sealing everything with surgical tape, but it still got in, and to a certain extent they got used to it and counted their blessings.

Those people had seen more hard work in a week than I had seen in my whole lifetime, and I had nothing but respect for them after an evening spent in their company. As for Higley, they told me that he eventually remarried and moved on, first sending for the two children that he had sent away before coming to Kansas. The Harlans hadn't heard from him again, but they had been told by a mutual acquaintance years later that he had died shortly after the death of his final wife, the cause of death said to be grief over her passing. That made me think of Goldie, and I felt anxious to get back to her.

So that was it. I had reached the final stop on my journey, and I was utterly convinced that I had found the home of "Home on the Range." I didn't feel the same pride that I had felt in Colorado when I thought that I had finished my work, but I felt a deeper sense of satisfaction knowing of a certainty that I had found the truth and that those kind people in Smith Center had earned their rightful place in the history of America's beloved song.

It was time for me to go home, but first I had to phone Dorothy. She took the news better than I thought she would, better than I would have. She said it was good that I told her myself instead of letting her read it in the papers, and I made her promise to visit Goldie and me in New York someday.

Goldie was sitting in her rocking chair by the big bay window when I arrived home, and she said she couldn't pick herself up to come and greet me because she was too fat. I put down my bags by the door and walked into the sitting room, where I remember her looking angelic in the light coming in from the window. I gave her a summary of my trip and took out the buffalo I had bought for her in Wichita, which she examined briefly then put aside. She didn't like it as much as I'd thought she would, and in the end it became mine, and I named it Brewster. It still sits on my desk and reminds me of that trip. As for Goldie and me, things changed after that. I tried harder to understand her, and she got some help and became a model mother to our son. Eventually I came to realize the part I had played in her unhappiness, but that's another story.

Whenever I speak about my life, the song comes up, and inevitably my listeners try to sing it, which is always amusing. I've yet to hear someone get it right, but I've also yet to meet someone who doesn't try. Among people of all ages, from all walks of life, everyone in America is familiar with at least the chorus, and how many songs can you say that of? Yes, it's woven right into the fabric of our nation's history, and I'm proud to say that my name is woven in there too, in some small way.

In the late 1940s, when celebrated American folklorist John A. Lomax put out his autobiography, *Adventures of a Ballad Hunter*, I learned the story behind one of the first recordings of "Home on the Range," for which he was responsible. In the summer of 1908, Lomax was engaged in an epic cross-country trip on horseback, with his Edison recording device strapped to the pommel of his saddle and the great horn lashed to the canter. In San Antonio, the old cavalier was directed to a saloon called The Road to Ruin, whose proprietor, a black man who had been a cook in the cow camps, was said to know many of the old cowboy songs. When Lomax arrived, the man apparently told him, "I'm drunk. Come back tomorrow." The next day he went back and recorded several songs, among them "Home on the Range." After that, Lomax had a blind music teacher from the Austin State School for the Blind do up the sheet music, which Lomax admits to altering slightly, according to his own tastes. Since the original cylindrical recording has crumbled into dust, we will never know how Lomax changed the song, but I like to think that it is another instance of how the ballad inspired people to put their own mark on it. Perhaps I would have taken a stab at it myself, if I were not such a clumsy poet.

In the years since I took that trip, I have continued to follow the evolution of "Home on the Range," keeping track of new versions that spring up, even the profane schoolyard variations that young people joke over. I think it's a shame that the song has gone into decline in recent years, because I believe that it has a lot to teach us about ourselves and our nation—what has been gained and what has been lost.

I keep pinned over my desk the earliest surviving print version of Higley's poem, and I have looked over that old issue so many times, pondering the nearly one hundred years of American history that have elapsed since the ink first met that page. The theme of the issue was "Westward the March of Empire Makes its Way," and next to Higley's poem is printed another, which I have read and reread almost as often. I will include it here as a conclusion to this report.

> I hear the tread of pioneers
> Of nations yet to be,
> The first low wash of waves where soon
> Shall roll a human sea.
>
> Behind the scared squaw's birch canoe,
> The steamer smokes and raves;

And city lots are staked for sale
Above old Indian graves.

The rudiments of Empire here,
Are plastic yet and warm;
The chaos of a mighty world
Is rounding into form.

1972
The Rusts

A DRY, HOT DAY IN ATHOL, Kansas. Pearl Hollis eats Fritos and plays solitaire on the bright blue counter of her kiosk. She hears a car coming, so she pulls out her compact and checks her makeup and teeth. She's been doing this a lot since she heard that Jesse is back; she has no way to know when she will see him.

A station wagon rolls in. Pearl leans back in her chair and licks her yellow fingers as she watches a middle-aged couple and their two children get out of the car. The man moves to the picnic table in the shade to try and refold a huge United States map. The sullen teenaged boy leans against the car's hood. The girl lopes toward Pearl, her hands low to the ground. The woman wipes sweat from her forehead with the back of her hand and fans herself with a brochure.

"Stop that, Val," she says as the girl reaches the kiosk and rears up like a prairie dog, her tongue wagging. Pearl ignores her, so she lopes over to the man, who is still unfolding and refolding the map. The woman approaches the kiosk.

"We're looking for the Home on the Range cabin," she says.

Pearl hands the woman the printed directions—a slip of paper with a crude drawing on it. The cabin is the only thing deemed worth seeing near Athol, apart from the fire truck on a Pierce Arrow chassis that's stored in the community hall, but no one comes for that. Tourists stop in Smith Center to sign their names in the rainproof box next to the monument that marks the geographical centre of the United States. After that, they come out here to see the place where a pioneer wrote the state song.

"Thank you, dear," the woman says. "Would you like a cold drink?"

Sometimes people give her drinks. Sometimes a sandwich or some candy. Sometimes a comment about her lonely job that's really directed at their families, like "Heck, I wish *I* could get a chance to hear *my*self think every now and then."

The woman is digging in a cooler in the back of the station wagon. "Purple or orange?"

"Purple," Pearl shouts.

"Shit," the man says, finally giving up and mashing the map together. The woman, looking embarrassed, passes Pearl a wet bottle of grape soda and goes to help her husband.

Pearl imagines them driving away in silence, first to the cabin, then back to their house, wherever that is. She wonders if they chose the way their lives are or if they are like everyone else she knows. Like her father, who works in the pork commissioner's office and rarely speaks about anything but his job and his gas grill. Like her mother, who does crosswords and cross-stitch all day, who worries so much about the opinions of others that she considers what the women at the checkout will think of her groceries. Like Dan Rust, Pearl's boyfriend, who will live every day of his life within a ten mile radius of the place he was born and never once let on how much he hates it.

After the family leaves, Pearl sits under the box elder by the highway to smoke a cigarette. She can see the Rusts' farm in the distance; she thinks how strange it is to imagine Jesse back there again. Normally on a hot day Dan would pick her up after work and they would go swimming in the lake, but today he has a heifer calving, so she will bike home alone. The farm is on her way, but she won't stop to see Dan and the calf. She has been avoiding the place since Jesse came back, because she doesn't want Dan to think she's looking for an excuse to see his brother. Instead, she waits for Jesse to come to her.

With Jesse, she was always waiting. Waiting for him to take her someplace, waiting for him to bring her home, waiting for the momentous thing that always seemed about to happen when he was around. When her family moved to Kansas, she had been unable to make friends. She'd never been an outgoing person, but when they'd lived in Minnesota, she had always had at least one or two friends. In Smith Center, though, she was lost. She tried at first to insinuate herself into a group by smiling at other girls in class or sitting next to people at lunch, but nothing worked, and soon she decided that it was better to stop trying than to continue looking so desperate.

She spent her lunch hours wandering around the school as

if she were on her way somewhere, hoping that no one would notice she was going in circles. After a while she told herself that she liked being alone and she didn't care if everyone thought she was weird or pathetic. She spent her breaks either reading or, more often, pretending to read while she was actually busy watching other kids being normal, trying to imagine her situation as an alien might, or someone from the future, so that she could convince herself that none of it was as important as it seemed.

Then one day Jesse came and sat next to her and asked what she was reading. She had never spoken to him before, but he was popular so she knew a lot about him, although she tried not to let on. He could have had any girl he wanted in that school, but for some reason she had never understood, he chose her, and from the beginning her gratitude was coloured by the terror of her new helplessness. She had spent so long convincing herself that she wanted to be alone, but almost immediately after that first conversation with Jesse she realized she'd been waiting her whole life for someone to see her the way he saw her, and she knew that she was bound to him no matter what he did or failed to do.

The night before he was supposed to leave for army training camp, the two of them lost their virginity together on an old blanket in the bed of his pickup truck. He'd had to explain everything for her, and she'd wondered how he knew. She remembers how his hands felt on her skin, how he looked at her the whole time as if he had some urgent question that needed answering, how everything was charged with the possibility that he would die in the war, how she wished that he could be less beautiful, because it was painful to want something so much. Afterward, he dropped her off at home, got drunk alone and drove his truck into a tree. He was found the next morning, and the volunteer fire department came and got him out.

Everyone said it was a miracle, because apart from some glass in his face, there wasn't a scratch on him. But soon they realized that he was damaged in other ways. He stopped wearing shoes and talked non-stop, saying crazy things no one understood. One morning he told his family they would probably never see him again, got on his bike and left. The bike was found in a ditch a week later, and they all thought he was dead until they got a letter saying he was working as a roadie for some band. After that, there was one more letter, which his mother wouldn't show Pearl, because she said it didn't make a lick of sense. Then there was a long silence, which Dan filled.

No one knows why Jesse has come home now. People say he's still as crazy as the day he left and has changed his name to Zeppelin or something. Most of them think he has come back for Pearl. She's sure that Dan thinks so as well, although he doesn't say it. He has never said anything against his brother, never complained about being left to take care of the farm while Jesse went off to discover himself. Only once he seemed to be warning her not to hold onto whatever ideas she might still have about Jesse. She'd been talking about travelling, having some new experiences, and he told her that she could learn about poison by taking poison, but it was much better to read about it in a book.

As she smokes and drinks her purple soda, Pearl imagines finding Jesse walking alone by the lake where they used to swim together on hot summer days. She imagines hugging him for a long time and him stroking her hair like he used to. He might suggest a swim, and afterward they would lie on the grass in their wet underwear and she would tell him that she sees it all differently now than she did before. At the time, the sudden change in him had frightened her, but now she has begun to understand that he was only saying the truth no one wanted to hear.

The day he got out of hospital she had gone to the junkyard with him. He wasn't supposed to, but she let him drive her mother's car. He wasn't supposed to get high, either, but she dutifully rolled joints for him and worked the gears when he told her to. In the junkyard, she waited while he filled a paper bag with whatever he could retrieve from the wreck. Clothes, cigarettes, eight-tracks. He brushed off the driver's seat with a magazine and sat down. The truck around him was completely crushed, apart from the tiny space where he sat. He put his hands on the wheel and grinned at Pearl through the shattered glass. She was horrified by how much the idea of his own death seemed to excite him, but thinking back on it now, it only makes her more determined to escape the drawn out dulling that has inhabited the lives of everyone else she knows. She feels such promise, knowing that he is there. Such hope that something is finally about to happen.

She checks her watch, takes a last drag on her cigarette before snuffing it out on the tree trunk. At the kiosk, she pulls down the sign, sweeps cigarette butts from the floor and locks the shutters and door. She takes her bike from the side of the building and begins to pedal slowly down the flat highway.

Sometimes when she is alone, she gives herself challenges, like "I must pass that mailbox before the next car passes me." They start out as silly things, but as the moment approaches she becomes convinced that something terrible will happen if she fails. Up ahead, she can see a crow pecking at something on the median, and she decides she has to pass the tree near the road to the Rust farm before the crow flies away. She pedals hard, tucks her chin down and coasts along the centre line. She watches as the crow pecks the body on the ground, looks up suddenly, circles around, goes back to pecking. As she comes closer to the tree, she becomes aware of movement around it. Turning away from the crow, she sees smoke rising up around the trunk. As she is about to pass the tree, she notices someone sitting cross-legged under it.

She hits her brakes. The crow flies away.

The sun is behind Jesse, casting him in silhouette, but she sees that his hair is long, and he's wearing a brown shirt that she recognizes as Dan's. Around his neck are four strands of beads. She feels a compulsion to cross herself as protection against whatever might happen because the crow flew away. She combines the quick series of motions with the movement of shielding her eyes against the afternoon sun and hopes that Jesse won't think she's doing it on his account, but he doesn't seem to have noticed her at all.

His eyes are half closed, and he is using a cupped hand to draw smoke over his body from a container he's holding in his other hand. He seems to be glowing from the places where the sun touches his face and body through the shadows of the leaves. She watches his hands, his arms, the muscles working under his skin. She recognizes that his are the same as Dan's hands, but seeing them performing this mysterious ritual makes her certain that she wants those hands—Jesse's hands—to touch her again. She feels a pang of guilt. Dan has done everything for her. He's accepted her despite her strangeness. He's made the world safe for her, finally. But as she watches Jesse do whatever he's doing, she thinks she has wasted too much time trying to be safe, and now it's almost too late to do anything else, but it's not too late yet.

Pearl lays her bike down on the side of the road and walks toward Jesse. She tries to make her footsteps quiet, to show respect. She thinks about his face that night before his accident, how carefully he arranged the blanket under her, how his weight felt along her body. When he puts down the container with the smoke, she expects him to turn and look at her, but instead he leans over something in front of him, caressing it and speaking in a low voice.

As she gets closer, she steps on some branches, to make sure he knows she's there. He leans back, his hands still on the thing in front of him, and begins to make noises like an Indian, *HEY-a-a-a-HEY-a-a-a*. She is so close now that he must know it. She thinks how often she found herself in this exact position when they were together. When he came to her, she was ready for anything he needed, but when she came to him, she had to wait. He always had a reason for it, but after a while she began to suspect that he was doing it on purpose, to keep her forever wanting more than he could give.

She stops walking. He stands, continuing to chant, and

she sees that the thing in front of him is a bird of some kind, maybe an owl. He stops chanting and stands quietly, his head bowed.

"Jesse," she says.

He kneels in front of the bird again and strokes its feathers, speaking under his breath. She wonders if she should leave, but she thinks that would be even more humiliating than being ignored, so she stays put while Jesse takes the tips of the bird's wings in each hand and lifts it up. She can see its collapsed face. Its beak and eyes are gone. He speaks to it, and Pearl strains to hear, but she can't make out his words. At last he places it tenderly on the ground and turns to her, and she sees that he has been crying.

"Hi," she says. He is looking directly into her eyes, and she tries to return his gaze, but it's unbearable having him look into her like that. "How have you been?" she says, looking at her hands, feeling idiotic. "I mean, how's California? I heard you were living there."

"Sit with us," he says. She smiles, hoping that he will say something normal, but he keeps watching her, and she feels naked and judged. She sits next to him, holding her knees to her chest and looking at the bird. He moves away a bit, and she feels hurt until she sees that he is reaching for something in his pocket. She edges further away from him as he takes out a knife and opens it.

"She brought me here," he says.

"What are you doing with that?" Again he doesn't answer, only smiles at her as he brings his knife to the place where the bird's right wing meets its body. Pearl gasps. He looks at her, and she wishes she hadn't shown her surprise, because she can see that it's what he wants.

"I had a dream that I was an owl flying over the Solomon River," he says as he works through the bone. "The next morning I found her outside my tent."

"You brought a dead owl all the way from California?"

He holds the severed wing up and looks at it in the sunlight.

"Like, in your backpack?"

"Yes."

"Didn't it smell?"

"I wrapped her in plastic."

Pearl wonders how she must look to him. The last time he saw her, she was seventeen years old. Does he notice the beginnings of wrinkles around her mouth, the visible veins on her thighs, the scar from the time she tried to open a tin can with a steak knife? She wonders if he still loves her, and she thinks that if he does his love would mean more than Dan's, because he has so many other people he could love.

"It's really good to see you again," she says. He doesn't react. "So, you live on like a commune in California?"

"I live on a farm," he says, working on the other wing now. The way he's being with her, as if he knew everything about her and there was no need to ask, makes her feel something she's often felt with Dan. It's as if he can easily read signs she can't even see, but the difference is that Dan never makes her feel that way on purpose.

"And you're going to do that forever?"

He props the owl and its severed wings against the tree trunk before looking at her again. "Pearl, you shouldn't stay here." He seems about to say more, but something behind her draws his attention. She follows his gaze to see Dan's truck coming down the long road from the farm, and she feels some urgency, realizing that this might be the last time she and Jesse are alone.

"Why did you come home, Jess?" she says.

"My name's Zephyr now," he says.

"Why?"

"Jess was never me."

Pearl turns again, and as they both watch Dan's truck coming toward them, she feels grateful for Dan, who is always the same.

"Why did you come home?" she says again.

"I already told you." He puts his hands behind him on the ground and leans back. "Also, to tell you the truth, I was getting sort of sick of the way things were going. I'm the only one who knows anything about farming, so after a while it was me nailing everything down and everyone else fucking off and all these lazy pricks hanging on. I needed to take a break to get some perspective."

"Why come here when you hate it so much?"

He looks at her again, and this time she stares back. "Before I left I know you thought I was all fucked up," he says. "But that was the most honest moment of my life, because my mind opened up and I saw reality as it is."

"There's no such thing as reality as it is," she says, and she is surprised by how annoyed she feels. She wonders if it's true that she was ever so in love with Jesse, or if she had just chosen to remember it that way.

"Yes there is," he says. "After my accident everybody made me feel like I was a freak, but when I left this shithole I found plenty of people tuned into the same exact thing I was tuning into, and I got that it's the world that's brain damaged, not me."

Dan has pulled over near them, and Pearl and Jesse stand to watch him get out of his truck.

"So I should be like you and leave behind the people who love me to go and live with a bunch of strangers and be the dope who does all the hard work?"

"God, Pearl," he says. "I'm only trying to explain to you that you have to get out of here, to encounter your freedom." Maybe there were only a few good times, she thinks. A few swims in the lake, that night in the back of his truck, and she turned them into a memory of a whole era, a whole person, who never existed.

Dan has started to jog toward them now. His overalls look muddy, and something shines in an arc around his head.

"What the hell is that?" Jesse says. Pearl squints. It looks like some kind of rope or chain, something metal.

"What, does he want to fight?" Jesse says. "I'm so sick of his tough guy bullshit. He thinks I came back here to steal you from him, can you believe that? All he thinks about is ownership. He's obsessed with it. I told him he can have the farm. He can have mom and dad's money. I don't want anything."

"There's nothing to have, Jesse. Don't you see?"

"I told you my name is Zephyr," he says. "And you're the one who doesn't see." His face is completely changed now, filled with contempt. "You can't even see what's right in front of your face."

Dan is swinging a short, thin chain like a lasso. His face is soaked with sweat. Pearl has never seen him like this, and she starts to laugh nervously, despite herself.

"Okay, motherfucker." Jesse holds up his fists. Pearl watches Dan's heaving chest, the sweat on his cheeks, the ridiculous swinging chain. His overalls are stained with dried blood, and Pearl realizes that it must be from the cow. He swings the chain faster as he gets closer. Jesse opens his fists and holds his hands up in front of his face.

Pearl screams as Dan's chain meets Jesse's hands, slicing first into his knuckles and then his left arm. Jesse is on Dan in a second, his hands in a chokehold around Dan's neck. Pearl tries to pull him off, but it's no use. She kicks dust at him. His hands are running with his own blood. His face is terrible. Dan's eyes bulge. Finally Jesse lets go, and Dan turns over, coughing in the dirt.

Jesse stands up and wipes his hands on his shirt. He leans forward, his palms on his knees, and tries to catch his breath. Pearl kneels next to Dan, who is holding his throat, and he leans into her chest and sobs.

Jesse hovers by them, but Pearl doesn't look at him.

"I'm sorry," Jesse says. He reaches out but doesn't touch his brother. "Dan, I'm sorry, okay?"

After she's sure that Dan is okay, Pearl leaves the brothers in the field. Neither of them follows or calls after her, and she doesn't look back. She rides until she's out of sight of them and then she stops, straddling her bike. She breathes deeply, her hand on her chest. She can still hear the sound of the chain hitting Jesse's hands and Dan choking and crying.

She considers how she feels, and she's surprised to find that she doesn't feel much of anything. It's as if a space is opening up inside her, and it's empty. It occurs to her that in high school her loneliness forced her into a strange bond with herself, a necessary solidarity with the pathetic creature that she was, which she lost when Jesse offered to shelter her under his wing. Now this cold, mysterious feeling is like being visited by an old friend. She knows it won't last, so she stays like that for a while, standing on the shoulder of the road, until she gets tired of thinking that way and rides her bike home through the near dark.

ESSAY

From "No Place" to Home

The Quest for a Western Home in Brewster Higley's
"Home on the Range"

IN THE SPRING OF 1935, New York attorney Samuel Moanfeldt set out on a road trip in search of the origins of the popular American folk song, "Home on the Range." The reason for his trip was a five hundred thousand dollar lawsuit filed by William and Mary Goodwin of Tempe, Arizona, who claimed that they had written the song—then the most popular song on the American airwaves—and were owed royalties in arrears for its broadcast on public radio.

Moanfeldt's investigation ended in Smith County, Kansas, where he found proof that the song had originated in the form of a poem written in 1872 by a pioneer doctor named Brewster Higley.[1] The case was closed, but Moanfeldt's report of his investigation revealed much about the song's history. For this, we are indebted to the Goodwins, without whose false claim of authorship this story might have been lost. However, the Goodwins were not unique in claiming authorship of one of America's favourite songs, a song that by the middle of the twentieth century was, as author Carl Biemiller writes, "as well known as daybreak."[2] By the time the Goodwins filed their suit, Kansas, Arizona and New Mexico had claimed "Home on the Range" as their own, and it

1 John A. Lomax, *Adventures of a Ballad Hunter* (New York: Hafner Publishing Co., 1971), 63.

2 Carl L. Biemiller, "The Land Sings Its History," *Country Gentleman*, July 1948, 79.

had been made official in the *Congressional Record* that the song had originated in Colorado.[3]

As word spread about the song's contested origins, the claims of authorship multiplied. In 1946, when American author Homer Croy went looking for more information about the song, he discovered that despite the fact that Moanfeldt had authenticated the song's authorship to the satisfaction of both the courts and authorities on American folk music, many Americans still claimed that they or someone they knew had written it.[4] "One claimant even showed up from the state of Washington," writes Croy, "where, so far as I know, no buffalo ever roamed."[5] Croy published a letter in the paper asking for information and was amazed by the responses he received: "Many of the authors said their father had written the famous song, for he had sung it to them when they were children and had told them he had written it; and in this way they were sincere and earnest; many sent ancient clippings and copies of diaries."[6]

The sense of ownership that so many Americans have felt for this song is a testament to its ability to evoke a deep and enduring ideal—the garden of the West—that mythic space beyond the frontier where Frederick Jackson Turner claimed that the American character was forged. Henry Nash Smith argued that American history was above all a story about the relationship between human beings and nature, or more specifically, the relationship between "American man and the American West."[7] Because "Home on the Range" was originally a pastoral poem, its adaptation over time reflects dominant themes in the relationship of the American people to the natural world. Because it emerged from a pioneer agrarian society at the edge of the frontier and was written in the twilight of an era that continues to haunt the

3 Homer Croy, *Corn Country* (New York: Duell, Sloan and Pearce, 1947), 164.

4 Kirke Mechem, *The Story of Home on the Range*, Kansas State Historical Society: *Kansas Historical Quarterly*, November 1949, 7.

5 Croy, *Corn Country*, 173.

6 Ibid., 166.

7 Henry Nash Smith, *Virgin Land: The American West as Symbol and Myth* (Cambridge: Harvard University Press, 1950), 187.

American imagination, the story of the song is also the story of the changing relationship between Americans and the American West. Its various messages and emphases reflect shifts both in dominant ideological conceptions of nature and the material realities of a changing American landscape.

In his essay "The Land Sings Its History," Biemiller argues that folk music can tell us as much about American history as any textbook.[8] "Home on the Range" is emblematic of this tradition. As is typical of folk music, it arose from obscure origins, was passed on orally, and has been revised and rearranged as it has travelled through time and across the American landscape. As a result, the evolution of the song provides a record of tensions between the lived realities and most cherished dreams of Americans from the late nineteenth century until today. "The land has sung its history," writes Biemiller,[9] and in the case of "Home on the Range," the constantly returned-to refrain is the quest for a home.

NO PLACE

Brewster Higley VI was born on November 23, 1823, in Rutland, Ohio. His father died before he was born and his mother died when he was a child. After his mother's death, he lived with his grandfather and then his sister.[10] He studied medicine in Indiana, where between 1849 and 1864 he married three different women, two of whom died.[11] There are few records of his early life, but testimonies of individuals connected to Higley, collected by historian Russell K. Hickman in 1949, paint a portrait of a lonely, troubled man who struggled with poverty and alcoholism. Margaret Carpenter, who knew

8 Biemiller, "The Land Sings Its History," 25.

9 Ibid., 79.

10 Mary Coffin Johnson, *The Higleys and Their Ancestry: An Old Colonial Family* (New York: Appleton and Company, 1896), 269.

11 Mechem, *Story of Home on the Range*, 10.

Higley when she was a child in Indiana, remembered him as a local oddity whose family was "as poor as Job's turkey."[12]

A Mrs. Smith, the niece of Higley's third wife, Catherine Livingstone, had mixed impressions of Higley. "Dr. Higley was considered a very fine doctor and was a brilliant man," she remembered.[13] Smith recalled Higley travelling on horseback to care for the families in the area, often accepting vegetables for payment. "But he let liquor get the better of him," she said.[14] Smith recalled being told by her father that her aunt—Higley's wife Catherine, who is listed in his biographical sketch in *The Higleys and Their Ancestry* as having died of "an injury"[15]—might have survived if she had received adequate medical attention, a statement that reflects very badly on Higley, a physician. Smith also claimed that when her aunt died, Higley did not pay the funeral expenses, leaving her family to cover the cost.[16]

In 1866 Higley married Mercy Ann McPherson, a widow with a young son.[17] This was by all accounts an unhappy marriage, and it is conspicuously absent from Higley's biographical sketch, likely at Higley's request.[18] In 1871 Higley sent his two youngest children to Illinois and left Indiana, making sure to keep his destination a secret. Hickman speculates that Higley might have headed West to escape the "poverty and misfortune" that he had suffered in Indiana. However, Higley took great pains to ensure that his whereabouts were unknown for years after he left, leading some to conclude that he fled to escape his marriage and any financial obligations he might have had to his wife.[19] Margaret Carpenter remembered his departure:

> He took a revolver from father, and said he was going to Rockford...I can remember father saying that he did not know where Higley had gone after he left this vicinity. Although no one

12 Russell K. Hickman, "The Historical Background of Home on the Range," *The Barlag Collection* (LaPorte County Historical Society), 12.

13 Ibid., 11.

14 Ibid., 11.

15 Johnson, *The Higleys and Their Ancestry*, 270.

16 Hickman, "Historical Background," 11.

17 Ibid., 14.

18 Ibid., 10–12.

19 Ibid., 14.

knew his whereabouts, Dr. Higley had often said he wanted
to go to Kansas, then a new country, and grow up with it.[20]

The passage of the Homestead Act in 1862 saw 718,930 homesteads
established on 96,495,414 acres of land in just forty years. Land was
cheap, and there was a constant call for settlers to come and reap the
West's resources, to "fulfill the promise of America."[21] The January 7,
1876, issue of the *Smith County Pioneer* calls for "500,000 or more men
and women—strong-minded, big-hearted, enterprising, persevering
and muscular people, afraid of nothing but wrong, to develop and
build up all the interests and institutions of this growing State."[22]
As was typical of immigration propaganda of the period, pioneers
were enticed with reference to a bounty of natural resources to be
exploited:

> Millions of acres of rich farming land invite the farmer's toil.
> The hill and bluff abound in rich building stone of the best
> kinds. Salt springs and marshes are wasting their riches for the
> want of more people and money. Beds of plaster of vast extent
> are ready to enrich the capitalist, farmer and mechanic. Stone-
> coal abounds in many places, and almost every week we hear
> of new veins being discovered. The rapids in our river furnish
> many good sites for all manufacturing purposes.[23]

20 Ibid., 11.

21 David Dary, *True Tales of Old-Time Kansas* (Lawrence: University Press of Kansas, 1984), 70.

22 "What Kansas Wants," *Smith County Pioneer*, January 7, 1976, 1.

23 Ibid.

But beyond responding to the lure of cheap land, it is
likely that Higley, like so many Americans before and
after him, saw the West as a regenerative landscape,
a place to begin again. A middle-aged alcoholic,
twice a widower, who had endured poverty and an
unhappy marriage, Higley had good reason to want
a new start, and the western frontier, that vast space
of cheap and sparsely populated land, offered a perfect
opportunity. As Elliott West writes, before it was

settled, the West was seen by European Americans as a place without a history, a pristine land of unlimited promise, upon which they could project their own fantasies. "In short," West writes, it was "No Place," the literal definition of utopia.[24]

Heroic tales of derring-do beyond the frontier fascinated some Americans, but it was to the agrarian West that Higley emigrated, along with thousands of others. These settlers made homes and began lives in a succession of new communities, planting crops and putting down roots.[25] "The image of this vast and constantly growing agricultural society in the continent's interior became one of the dominant symbols of nineteenth-century American society," writes Henry Nash Smith. "[A] collective representation, a poetic idea ... that defined the promise of American life."[26] And because this "poetic idea" expressed the greatest aspirations of the young nation and offered a hero in the form of the pioneer farmer, it assumed the quality of myth—the myth of the garden—which had its roots in Europe but took on new life and meaning on the North American continent.[27]

THE SOLOMON VALE

Higley spent his first winter in Kansas living in a boarding house before taking up a claim on the banks of the Beaver River in Smith County, where he was to spend the next three years, living in a one-room dugout and working as a saddlebag physician for the surrounding settlers.[28] No stranger to privation, he adapted quickly to the difficult life,[29] and he was remembered as an excellent doctor whose skills were highly valued. "He truly was a prairie physician," writes Croy; he attended nearly a hundred cases of

24 Elliott West, *The Way to the West: Essays on the Central Plains* (Albuquerque: University of New Mexico Press, 1995), 163.

25 Smith, *Virgin Land*, 123.

26 Ibid., 123.

27 Ibid., 124.

28 Margaret Nelson, *Home on the Range* (Toronto: Ryerson Press, 1947), 60.

29 Croy, *Corn Country*, 175.

typhoid in one year and often had to perform amputations with his handsaw and no anesthetic.[30] Higley's friend W.H. Nelson wrote of the doctor, "[N]o night was too dark or trail too dim to deter him from answering a demand for service, and there are no doubt many yet living in Smith County who owe him a debt of never ending gratitude for his timely medical attention."[31]

While living in Kansas, Higley often wrote down his thoughts and impressions in poetic form. He never sought to make money from his writing but enjoyed it as a hobby and a therapeutic form of personal expression.[32] Of his surviving writings, including a nine-page poem dedicated to "Dryden, Eng. Poet" and three songs, his favourite, according to his son, Brewster Higley VII, was "Army Blue," which he claimed to have written while living in Union Mills, Indiana.[33]

In 1872, Higley wrote a poem that went on to become "Home on the Range." Entitled "Oh, Give Me a Home Where the Buffalo Roam," the poem was first published in Higley's local Kansas newspaper the following year. The words were as follows:

Oh, give me a home where the buffalo roam
Where the deer and the antelope play,
Where never is heard a discouraging word
And the sky is not clouded all day.

Oh, give me the gale of the Solomon vale,
Where light streams with buoyancy flow,
On the banks of the Beaver, where seldom if ever
Any poisonous herbage doth grow.

Oh, give me the land where the bright diamond sand
Throws light from the glittering stream,
Where glideth along the graceful white swan,
Like a maid in her heavenly dream.

30 Ibid., 175.

31 Hickman, "Historical Background," 16.

32 Ibid., 18.

33 Croy, *Corn Country*, 174–75.

I love these wild flowers in this bright land of ours;
I love, too, the curlew's wild scream.
The bluffs of white rocks and antelope flocks
That graze on our hillsides so green.

How often at night, when the heavens are bright,
By the light of the glittering stars,
Have I stood there amazed and asked as I gazed
If their beauty exceeds this of ours.

The air is so pure the breezes so light,
The zephyrs so balmy at night.
I would not exchange my home here to range
Forever in azure so bright.[34]

There are varying accounts of the moment of the poem's conception.
Margaret Nelson, whose 1947 work seems to reflect her fantasies
of pioneer life more than the events of Higley's, writes a florid
account of that moment. Providing each line with a corresponding
environmental inspiration, Nelson writes that Higley was "suddenly
overcome with emotions" as he sat in the door of his log cabin
watching "the immense expanse of azure blue sky" and thinking of
"the charm of the bright days," "the air, like a gentle but mighty fan,"
"the happy, carefree settlers so buoyant and full of life," marvelling
at the plant life and abundance of wildlife roaming freely about him.
"Were we overlooking a part of Heaven right on earth?" Nelson's
Higley asks himself.[35]

Nelson continues her depiction of the scene that Higley describes
by establishing what it *isn't*, distinguishing the ideal
West from the "shallow" and "artificial" East in
Higley's mind.[36] Writing from an era in which the
robust Anglo-Saxon male in the austere western
landscape had emerged as the symbol of the American

34 Mechem, *Story of Home on the Range*, 17.

35 Nelson, *Home on the Range*, 134–37.

36 Ibid., 154–55.

ideal of democracy and self-reliance, Nelson introduces Higley as "a lone man, on his horse, traveling under the bright stars … the moonlight on the prairie bathing the world in luminous splendor… 'Oh, God,' he said, 'there is comfort out here in the open, away from the shallow and the artificial things of life. This is all the stimulant a man needs.'"[37]

In the same passage, Nelson explicitly promotes the notion that cities are the domain of selfishness, vice and iniquity, while rural landscapes attract and engender virtuous, honest and hardworking people. "He had taken care of the ailing indigents in the crowded cities," Nelson writes of Higley, and "they had aroused his sympathy, but never his deep respect and admiration" as the pioneers on the frontier did.[38]

The east/west dichotomy that Nelson creates reflects a common attitude of the time. In a 1939 *New York Times* article entitled "A New Yorker Rediscovers the West," J. Donald Adams gives voice to this notion of the constitutional superiority of westerners. Travelling westward across the continent, Adams perceives a significant cultural shift, a "deep-seated difference in spirit, in the attitude toward daily living."[39] Like others before him, Adams attributes this change in spirit to the promise and harshness of the landscape and to the adventurousness and hardiness of the people who settled this difficult region. "The West was born out of optimism," Adams writes. "And the strain has not become perceptibly diluted."[40]

Nelson presents the West as a "heaven on earth" in contrast to the "crowded" and "artificial" cities. This is a reflection of the cultural mores of the time in which she was writing, a time in which the western was well-established as a popular cultural form in both film and pulp fiction. "The western is the closest thing we have to a national myth," writes Elliott West.[41] And Nelson's depiction of Higley's life in Kansas is an example of how myths can replace historical facts.

37 Ibid., 154–55.

38 Ibid., 155.

39 J. Donald Adams, "A New Yorker Rediscovers the West," *New York Times*, October 15, 1939, 10.

40 Ibid., 21.

41 West, *Way to the West*, 164.

Like other myths, it is a highly manipulated story that packs a potent emotional punch, which has been used by successive generations "as a blank screen where they can project and pursue their fantasies," thus obscuring historical realities.[42]

Seen from another perspective, however, Nelson's extravagant account may in fact have been in keeping with the spirit of Higley's poem, as other reports of its writing suggest. A.E. Daniels, who was a child at the time the poem was written and a neighbour of Higley's, claimed in a 1946 interview that the song was written while Higley sat on a log outside his dugout waiting to shoot a deer. When no deer came, Daniels said, Higley decided to write a poem instead, to get down the feelings and sensations that had come over him as he observed the beauty of the landscape.[43]

People who lived in Kansas at the time the poem was written have pointed out that much of the environment described in Higley's poem could not have been present for Higley to see. The buffalo had ceased to roam in that area shortly before Higley arrived[44] and critics have questioned whether it is plausible that there were deer, antelope and especially wild swans as late as 1872.[45] "How that swan ever got into Beaver Creek I don't know," writes Croy. "The old doctor must have brought her from Indiana."[46] A contemporary of Higley's said, "I might add that at that time there was antelope [in Kansas] in plentiful numbers, also the curlew was there, but *not nary a dang swan*! Buffalo had been gone about three years."[47]

Of course, there is no way to rule out the possibility of Higley having spotted a swan or buffalo during that period, but taken together, the scene that he has described is perfect to the point of implausibility. The landscape that Higley has created in his poem is an ideal meeting of benevolent natural forces, a perfect and peaceful "garden of the West."

42 Ibid.

43 Croy, *Corn Country*, 169.

44 Ibid., 168.

45 Mechem, *Story of Home on the Range*, 18.

46 Croy, *Corn Country*, 172.

47 Lomax, *Adventures*, 63.

> I am looking rather seedy now while holding down my claim,
> And my vittles are not always of the best;
> And the mice play shyly 'round me as I nestle down to rest
> In my little old sod shanty on the plain.[48]

— THE LITTLE OLD SOD SHANTY ON THE PLAIN

For settlers like Higley, life was hard and the skies were often cloudy. Droughts, sandstorms and plagues of grasshoppers made pioneer life a constant struggle.[49] But Higley's poem ignores these hard truths, recording only the best attributes of a landscape that was already disappearing as he wrote. Without even a hint of the ambivalence and social critique that played out in other nineteenth-century pastoral literature, Higley's is a sentimental and unsophisticated poem in the pastoral mode of the English poets he admired.[50]

However, because the myth of the garden had undergone a significant change after it was imported to North America—a change that was reflected in a key distinction between European and American pastoral poetry—the depiction of nature in Higley's poem differs in at least one respect from depictions characteristic of the European pastoral. During the American Revolution, the basis of the myth was reworked, and what was in Europe a literary ideal or utopian dream became an insisted-upon reality in post-revolutionary American literature.[51] Annette Kolodny argues that "the earliest explorers and settlers in the New World can be said to have carried with them a 'yearning for paradise,'" and early American writing frequently asserted the realization of this dream of paradise, or what Kolodny calls "the soul's home."[52] In this early American literature,

48 John A. Lomax, *Cowboy Songs and Other Frontier Ballads* (London: Macmillan, 1938), 405.

49 Dary, *True Tales of Old-Time Kansas*, 71.

50 Nelson, *Home on the Range*, 258.

51 Smith, *Virgin Land*, 127.

52 Annette Kolodny, *The Lay of the Land: Metaphor as Experience and History in American Life and Letters* (Chapel Hill: University of North Carolina Press, 1975), 4.

the country is portrayed as a maternal landscape, abundant and nurturing, the return to nature offering reentry to this "soul's home"—the womb of Mother Nature.

Kolodny goes on to argue that the human impulse to project feminine characteristics onto the landscape in the "land as woman" paradigm was "a reactivation of what we now recognize as universal mythic wishes" to return to the maternal embrace. However, the difference in this case was that in American literature, the wished-for paradise had become the claimed reality.[53] As a result, Kolodny writes, "every word written about the New World [was touched] with the possibility that the ideally beautiful and bountiful terrain might be lifted forever out of the canon of pastoral convention and invested with the reality of daily experience."[54] Kolodny argues that by understanding this distinction between the American and European pastoral impulse we can make sense of the disparity between idealized literary depictions of life in America and the historical reality of the hardships endured during the period of settlement.[55]

Higley's poem fits into the American pastoral paradigm by conflating the real and the ideal into a portrait of a dream landscape, presented not as a promised or wished-for place but as an actual place that the author "would not exchange" for any other. And, as Kolodny argues, the willful imaginative creation of an idyllic landscape only became more attractive in the face of evidence to the contrary, because the belief that the ideal environment was possible helped settlers to overcome the hardships of their lives on the frontier.[56] Higley's poem, argues Hickman, can be seen as an "exaltation of spirit, an expression of hope for better days ahead."[57] And in this hope Higley was not alone—Croy maintains that "Home on the Range" "had the spirit of the early settlers better than any other song I had ever heard."[58]

53 Ibid., 5–6.
54 Ibid., 6.
55 Ibid.
56 Ibid., 154.
57 Hickman, "Historical Background," 22.
58 Croy, *Corn Country*, 164.

In 1873 Higley's poem was published in the *Smith County Pioneer*. The poem became instantly popular with the newspaper's readership for its celebration of the beauty of the land they loved and its optimism about the prospects of a good life there.[59] According to Margaret Nelson, many families pasted the clipping on the walls of their cabins and dugouts, where Higley's words helped to "cheer the struggling homesteaders on their way, and [drive] away the gloom and the loneliness of the next few years."[60]

The next time the poem was published was in 1874 in the *Kirwin Chief* in Phillips County, Kansas, alongside J.C. Greenleaf's "On Receiving an Eagle's Quill from Lake Superior," under the slogan "Westward the March of Empire Makes Its Way."[61] In this version, the poem had received a new name, "My Western Home," apparently at Higley's request.[62] Two years later, in 1876, the poem was reprinted in the same publication.[63] The *Chief* version is slightly different from the *Pioneer* version, with at least three changes worth noting here. First, the word "seldom" replaced "never" in the third line of the first stanza, a change that did not appear when the *Chief* printed the poem in 1874. This subtle alteration suggests a movement toward a more realistic depiction of life in the West. Secondly, the *Chief* reprint included the refrain from the song version, perhaps a nod to the song's growing popularity. Finally, the *Chief* retained the local references to Beaver Creek and the Solomon River but inserts mountains into the last line of the penultimate verse in the place of Higley's "hillsides"—a much more likely sight in Kansas.[64] This addition is a reflection of the distance the poem had already covered in the two years since it was written.

The occasion of the *Kirwin Chief* 1876 reprint was to contest yet another claim to authorship. "My Western Home" had been published earlier

59 Nelson, *Home on the Range*, 188.
60 Ibid.
61 Croy, *Corn Country*, 167.
62 Hickman, "Historical Background," 19.
63 Mechem, *Story of Home on the Range*, 7.
64 Ibid., 23.
65 Ibid., 7.

that year in the *Stockton News* under the title "My Home in the West," with a woman named Emma Race cited as the author.[65] This reprint is the first example of contested authorship leading to the preservation of the song's history, because it has become the earliest surviving version, as Higley's original was burned in a wagon fire and the 1873 *Pioneer* version apparently disappeared during the 1934 court case regarding the poem's authorship.[66] In rebuttal, the editor of the *Kirwin Chief* wrote a front-page editorial under the title "PLAGIARISM," which included a reprinting of "My Western Home," asking readers to compare Higley's version with Race's, which he says is identical apart from two words. The editorial ended by asking the editor of the *Stockton News* to "look to his laurels, as he will find plenty of people who are willing to profit by the brain work of others."[67]

At this point, it is worth exploring the possibility that Brewster Higley was not the original author of the poem. When folklorist John A. Lomax Sr. first read an account of the origins of "Home on the Range," he responded with skepticism. Turning to his extensive records on American folk music, he claimed to have found a letter from a Texan who said he had sung the song as early as 1867, five years before Higley is believed to have written it.[68] According to Higley's son, Brewster Higley VII, Higley was not especially proud of "Home on the Range," and he was not concerned about other claims to its authorship.[69] Apparently, of all the songs and poems Higley wrote, his favourite was "Army Blue," a song that he claimed to have written at the close of the Civil War. However, Hickman discovered that the song was a traditional standard at West Point Military Academy as early as 1865, leading him to question Higley's claim to its authorship.[70] Lomax's evidence is unsubstantiated, and even if Higley did not write "Army Blue," that fact alone would not be proof that he did not write

66 Croy, *Corn Country*, 167–69.

67 Mechem, *Story of Home on the Range*, 7.

68 John A. Lomax and Alan Lomax, *Folk Song: U.S.A.* (New York: Duell, Sloan and Pearce, 1947), 198.

69 Croy, *Corn Country*, 175.

70 Hickman, "Historical Background," 18.

161

"Home on the Range," but it would call into question the legitimacy of his claims to authorship in general.

Another source that brings Higley's authorship into question is the poem itself. In the *Pioneer* the second line of the third stanza is "where light streams with buoyancy flow." In the *Chief*, the line has been changed to "where *life* streams with buoyancy flow." Composer Kirke Mechem argues that neither of these was the author's intention, and therefore neither newspaper used the author's copy as a source. In both cases the line is "a nonsense line, such as we find in many folk songs, the corruption resulting from learning the song by ear."[71] Mechem suggests that the original line was—"where *live* streams with buoyancy flow"—the word *live* referring to "living water," both a Biblical term and a term commonly used by pioneers to describe running or spring-fed streams—something very important for people so dependent on agriculture.[72]

While Mechem makes a good case, he does not explore the possibility that his claim might imply that Brewster Higley was not the poem's author. When the poem appeared in the *Pioneer*, Higley was the assistant editor of the paper,[73] a fact that reduces the likelihood that the song as it appeared was not a reflection of his intentions. Further, because the title of the poem was changed for the *Chief* reprint on Higley's suggestion, it is likely that he had contact with the editor and could have requested a correction to the line if it had not been what he intended. While it is possible that he made this correction but was misunderstood (*live* could easily have been mistaken for *life*, and the *Chief* version does include other words not in Higley's original, as outlined earlier), this discrepancy inspires some doubt: Higley could have copied down the poem based on a mishearing of another, earlier version.

71 Mechem, *Story of Home on the Range*, 17.

72 Ibid.

73 Croy, *Corn Country*, 167.

Despite all of this, the evidence for Higley's authorship remains strong, and certainly no rival claims enjoy anything like the wealth of support his has, as Moanfeldt's report attests. However, even if Higley were not the author, that would not rule out the possibility that he believed himself to be. As the number of claims to authorship indicate, the poem expressed the American cultural dream life so well and people identified with it to such an extent, they may have sincerely believed that they had written it themselves. "Where will the trail end?" Lomax writes. "My guess is that it goes far back beyond Kansas and Texas, as well, into the big songbag which the folk have held in common for centuries."[74]

HOME ON THE RANGE

While the first phase of the poem's written transmission was carried out by small Kansas newspapers without much fanfare, another event set off radical changes that have shaped the story of the poem as we know it today. The dissemination of "Oh, Give Me a Home Where the Buffalo Roam" began when Higley's friend, Trube Reese, discovered the poem between the pages of a book in Higley's dugout. Reese persuaded Higley to have the poem put to music, leading Higley to give the poem to fiddler Dan Kelley, who composed music for his lyrics.[75] The most significant change brought upon the poem by being set to music was the addition of a refrain, apparently included at the suggestion of Judge Harlan, a partner in Kelley's Harlan Brothers Orchestra.[76] The refrain went like this:

A home, a home where the deer and the antelope
    play,
Where never is heard a discouraging word
And the sky is not clouded all day.[77]

While Nelson describes Kelley writing the music for the new song in the same kind of florid detail she used to describe Higley writing the words, Mechem argues

74 Lomax and Lomax, *Folk Song: U.S.A.*, 198.

75 Mechem, *Story of Home on the Range*, 6.

76 Nelson, *Home on the Range*, 168.

77 Mechem, *Story of Home on the Range*, 16.

that it is unlikely that Kelley would have written down the music,[78] and would instead have memorized it and played it often.[79] There is no known record of the original sheet music.[80]

The adaptation of Higley's poem into a folk song radically influenced the course of its history. Because folk music is generally learned by ear and passed orally from singer to singer, it is almost impossible for the original to remain unchanged. Folk songs are constantly adapted by the places and preoccupations of the people who sing them, as well as by simple mishearing or misinterpretation.[81] Therefore, Higley and Kelley's making "Oh, Give Me a Home Where the Buffalo Roam" into a song opened the poem up to unlimited possibilities of dissemination and revision, in the folk tradition.

The early settlers imported many Anglo-Saxon ballads from Europe that have since been adapted into American folksongs. However, Biemiller argues that only the songs that were "made on the site," songs written in America, truly reflect the development of the nation.[82] In the case of the western frontier, isolation, loneliness, and in many cases, illiteracy led to an outpouring of expression in the form of song.[83] As John A. Lomax writes, "[T]he frontier has been beaten back to the accompaniment of singing," and the songs that this period produced are a testament to the conditions and aspirations of pioneer life.[84]

"Oh, Give Me a Home Where the Buffalo Roam," first performed by Cal Harlan and the Harlan Brothers Orchestra in the town of Harlan, Kansas, in 1873, quickly became a favourite.[85] Played at every gathering and celebration, in no time it was known by almost everyone.[86] As Margaret Nelson writes, the song "spread over the country almost

78 Ibid.

79 Many early listeners noted that the tune sounded remarkably similar to a traditional church song, "Home of the Soul" (Wayne Gard, *The Chisholm Trail* [Norman: University of Oklahoma Press, 1954], 249; Lomax, *Adventures*, 64), suggesting yet another example of possible (and perhaps unintentional) plagiarism.

80 Ibid.

81 Biemiller, "The Land Sings Its History," 77.

82 Ibid.

83 Lomax, *Cowboy Songs*, xxv.

84 John A. Lomax and Alan Lomax, *American Ballads and Folk Songs* (New York: Dover Publications, 1934), xxvi; Lomax, *Cowboy Songs*, xxv.

85 Croy, *Corn Country*, 169.

86 Mechem, *Story of Home on the Range*, 31.

by magic."[87]Mechem notes that "nothing in the history of the song is so remarkable as the way it spread from one singer to another until it was known everywhere on the Western frontier."[88] He quotes one writer as saying, "With neither printed words nor music, far out on the unsheltered plain, 'Home on the Range' became a song hit 1,500 miles west of Broadway!"[89]

The seemingly instantaneous popularity of the song was owed to the immense amount of human movement characteristic of that place and time. While the railroads and pioneers pushed the frontier westward, ever-expanding numbers of cattle farming outfits swelled the cattle trails, and buffalo hunters drove south for the hunt.[90] According to Mechem,

> [o]nly the year before the song was written the Santa Fe reached Dodge City. Almost overnight the town became the largest cattle market in the world and the shipping center of the Southwest. The hunters who exterminated the buffalo here marketed several million dollars worth of hides and meat. Hundreds of wagon trains carried supplies to Western towns and army posts. By 1875, three years later, nearly all the cattle trails led to Dodge; in 1884 Texas drovers alone brought 106 herds numbering 300,000 head.[91]

The last point turned out to be of greatest significance to the history of the song, which has become "the national anthem of the cowboy," despite the fact that in its original form it had nothing to do with this stock western figure.[92] As Mechem writes, "[I]t is perhaps more than a coincidence that the life of Dodge City as a great cattle market, from the early 1870's to the middle 1880's, approximated that of the first life of 'Home on the Range.'"[93] Where the trails converged and cowboys met, songs were shared at social gatherings and sung on the drive during the day

87 Nelson, *Home on the Range*, 170.

88 Mechem, *Story of Home on the Range*, 11.

89 Ibid.

90 Ibid.

91 Ibid.

92 Jim Bob Tinsley, *He Was Singin' This Song* (Orlando: University Presses of Florida, 1981), 214.

93 Mechem, *Story of Home on the Range*, 11.

165

and to dispel loneliness and soothe restless cattle at night.[94] As these songs were passed along, they were altered according to singer and place.[95] Verses were added and taken away, local references were dropped and new ones included.

Above all, "Home on the Range" owes its popularity to American cowboys.[96] However, it was not only the nomadic lifestyle of these men that accounts for their contribution to the song's popularity. As with its other interpreters, the cowboys altered the song in ways that reveal yet another image of the "Western Home." Of these, the most enduring is the change in the penultimate line of the poem that made "range" part of a prepositional phrase instead of an infinitive, replacing "I would not exchange my home here to range" with "I would not exchange my home on the range."[97] Thus, rather than being committed to a specific home as a physical place "here" in Smith County, Kansas, the range itself becomes the home. In contrast to the sedentary settlers staking claims, the rootless cowboys expanded the concept of home to include all of the range country across which they wandered. This slight alteration, along with the removal of local references, gave the song its present title and transformed it from a ballad about a specific locale to one that could apply to every westerner.[98]

94 Hickman, "Historical Background," 1.

95 Tinsley, *He Was Singin' This Song*, xiii.

96 Hickman, "Historical Background," 1.

97 Mechem, *Story of Home on the Range*, 23.

98 Ibid.

99 Douglas B. Green, *Singing in the Saddle: The History of the Singing Cowboy* (Nashville: Country Music Foundation Press and Vanderbilt University Press, 2002), 3.

COLORADO HOME

The nineteenth-century gold rushes amplified both literal and imaginative interactions with the western frontier.[99] Scores of settlers headed west in the hopes of striking it rich. "In effect," writes Kolodny, "the new nation had entered its adolescence, leaving behind … the configuration of the Mother and making of the landscape, instead, a field for exercising sexual mastery and assertive independence."[100] The hero of this version of the western myth was not the yeoman farmer tirelessly tilling and sowing the soil but the mining man who (in theory, at least) earned his fortune overnight, reaching his pan into a riverbed and coming up rich.[101] He did not make his home in a sod house on the prairie, but in a crowded cabin or dugout, with other miners seeking their fortunes.

In the winter of 1885, while the song's popularity as a cowboy ballad was still in its infancy, four young prospectors in Leadville, Colorado, were snowed in one night in a cabin they nicknamed the Junk Lane Hotel. These men—Bob Swartz, Bill McCabe, Bingham Graves, and Jim Foutz—were musicians, and they often sang, played and wrote music together to pass the time during the long winter months.[102] "They make this their headquarters," Bob Swartz wrote of his companions in a letter home. "Most any night, 11, 12 or 1 o'clock you can look in at old Junk and hear the band going or singing with the banjo or a card game going on."[103] On this particular winter evening, the men composed a song they called "Colorado Home," which went on to become an instant favourite among their prospecting friends.[104] In a letter to his parents dated February 15, 1885, Swartz recounted the events of that evening:

> We have originated a new song, music and all, and it's creating quite a stir among the boys all around. I got up the tune and Bill most of the words, but we all had a hand in it as the cabin was full that night and everybody helped make it up. If it keeps on going it will become a popular western song.[105]

Swartz included with the letter both the lyrics and music, unknowingly producing the earliest known

100 Kolodny, *Lay of the Land*, 133.

101 Ibid.

102 Don L. Griswold and Jean Harvey Griswold, *History of Leadville and Lake County, Colorado: From Mountain Solitude to Metropolis* (Boulder: University Press of Colorado, 1996), 2:1623.

103 Kenneth S. Clark, "Colorado Home Prospectors' Song: The Original of 'Home on the Range'" (New York: Paul Pioneer Music Corporation, 1934), 4.

104 Griswold and Griswold, *History of Leadville*, 2:1623.

105 Clark, "Colorado Home," 4.

copy of the musical score to "Home on the Range."[106] The lyrics, however, were dramatically different from Higley's poem:[107]

Oh! Give me a home, where the buffalo roam,
And the deer and the antelope play.
Where seldom is heard a discouraging word
And the sky is not cloudy all day.

Oh! Give me the hill, and the ring of the drill
In the rich silver ore in the ground
And give me the gulch, where the miners can sluice
And the bright yellow gold can be found.

Oh! Give me the gleam, of the swift mountain stream
And the place where no Hurricanes blow
And give me the Park with the prairie dog bark,
And the mountains all covered with snow.

Oh! Give me the mines, where the prospector finds
The gold in its own native land.
With the hot springs below, where the sick people go
And camp on the banks of the Grand.

Oh! Show me the camp, where the prospectors tramp
And business is always alive.
Where dance halls come first, and faro banks burst,
And every saloon is a dive.

Oh! Give me my steed, and the gun that I need
To shoot game for my own cabin home;
And give me the light of the campfire at night
And the wild Rocky Mountains to roam.[108]

106 Griswold and Griswold, *History of Leadville*, 2:1624.

107 William and Mary Goodwin also claimed authorship of Swartz's version of Higley's poem. In 1915 they published the exact verses as they appear here through Balmer and Weber Music House Company in St. Louis, also with the title "Arizona Home."

108 Clark, "Colorado Home," 5.

Shortly after they wrote the song, the Junk Lane musicians went their separate ways, scattering to various parts of the West and taking the song with them.[109] "Colorado Home" went on to enjoy great popularity and even spawned its own imitation, "Oh, Give Me the Hills," which was recorded in 1903 near Idaho Springs, Colorado.[110]

The popularity of "Colorado Home," and the insistence by various parties until as late as 1945 that the song was a Colorado original,[111] is proof of how well the song portrayed that time and place as it wanted to see itself, a landscape rich in natural resources that are simply there for the taking. Instead of the "bright diamond sand," the "gale of the Solomon vale," and the "wild flowers," the prospector asked for "the hill and the ring of the drill" and "the mines where the prospector finds / The gold in its own native land." The land was transformed from a source of comfort and awe to a source of material wealth to be exploited. Thus, "Colorado Home" offers yet another vision of life in the West.

Although "Colorado Home" is clearly a variation on Higley's poem, this does not necessarily mean that Swartz and his friends knowingly plagiarized the song. As late as 1930, when "Home on the Range" was already popular on the radio, Swartz reiterated his claim to authorship in a reply to a birthday card in which his sister had enclosed his original 1885 letter with the lyrics of the song:

> I showed the letter to about 20 on my shift at the Round House that was interested…[S]ome of them didn't believe me some time ago, when I told them that some one was singing a song I wrote 50 years ago over the radio. And when I let them read the old letter, they were surprized and convinsed [*sic*]. It done me good to show it to them.[112]

It is quite possible that Swartz was sincere. Just as Higley and Kelley may have unconsciously drawn on

109 Ibid.

110 Tinsley, *He Was Singin' This Song*, 215.

111 Mechem, *Story of Home on the Range*, 4.

112 Clark, "Colorado Home," 5.

outside influences, the Junk Lane musicians may have been unaware of the extent to which they borrowed from an earlier version of a song that by that time had already entered into the American consciousness as an expression of a common and deeply felt sentiment. And rather than exonerate the Junk Lane composers on the grounds of unconscious plagiarism, it might be more appropriate to praise them for their contribution to the evolution of the song, which in the spirit of the folk tradition can be seen as a process of which adaptation and revision are fundamental aspects.

THE ROAD TO RUIN

In 1908 John A. Lomax travelled to San Antonio, Texas, with his Edison dictating machine looking for locals who were known to have folk songs committed to memory. He was directed to The Road to Ruin, a saloon where he met the African American proprietor he called Bill Jack McCurry. McCurry was a former cow camp cook and knew several cowboy songs by heart, which he allowed Lomax to record on a wax cylinder. One of the songs McCurry sang that day was "Home on the Range," and the recording was used to create a score.[113] Two years later, the song appeared in Lomax's *Cowboy Songs and Other Frontier Ballads*.[114]

113 Tinsley, *He Was Singin' This Song*, 214.

114 Mechem, *Story of Home on the Range*, 25.

115 Some changes also reflect the personal preferences of John Lomax, who admits to "rephras[ing] some unmetrical lines" (Lomax, *Adventures*, 62).

The song as sung by McCurry in 1908 is a historical snapshot, a freeze frame of a fluid process, reflecting some of the changes that had taken place in the thirty-seven years since the song was composed.[115] The lyrics of the McCurry/Lomax version are as follows:

Oh, give me a home where the buffalo roam,
Where the deer and the antelope play,

Where seldom is heard a discouraging word
And the skies are not cloudy all day.

Home, home on the range,
Where the deer and the antelope play;
Where seldom is heard a discouraging word
And the skies are not cloudy all day.

Where the air is so pure, the zephyrs so free,
The breezes so balmy and light,
That I would not exchange my home on the range
For all of the cities so bright.

The red man was pressed from this part of the West
He's likely no more to return,
To the banks of Red River where seldom if ever
Their flickering camp-fires burn.

How often at night when the heavens are bright
With the light from the glittering stars
Have I stood here amazed and asked as I gazed
If their glory exceeds that of ours.

Oh, I love these wild flowers in this dear land of ours
The curlew I love to hear scream,
And I love the white rocks and the antelope flocks
That graze on the mountain-tops green.

Oh, give me a land where the bright diamond sand
Flows leisurely down the stream;
Where the graceful white swan goes gliding along
Like a maid in a heavenly dream.[116]   116 Ibid., 24–25.

In the years since the song was written, the closing of the frontier had transformed the way America experienced and imagined its environment. By 1890 Frederick Jackson Turner had declared that there was not enough unsettled western land left to constitute a frontier.[117] In his essay, "The Significance of the Frontier in American History," Turner argued: "the existence of an area of free land, its continuous recession, and the advance of American settlement westward, explains American development."[118] Thus, Turner wrote, the closing of the frontier "[marked] the closing of a great historic movement."[119]

If, as Turner said, all the virtues and conditions—liberty, democracy, opportunity—that made America *America* were produced by the existence of free land, then presumably these virtues were under threat once the frontier was closed.[120] Without the purifying effects of the frontier, Turner implied, America would become as congested and oppressive as Europe.[121] The implications of Turner's observations were evident in the amendments and additions to "Home on the Range" that were made in the years between the poem's conception in 1872 and its reification in print in 1910.

Apart from the previously explored shift of the word "range" from verb to noun in the third verse (which was the final verse in the original), another important change made during the years cowboys spent tinkering with the song was the modification of the final line of this verse from "forever in azure so bright" to "for all of the cities so bright." The song's singer is now committed to the range as his home, and rather than being unwilling to exchange this home for heaven, the singer is now unwilling to exchange it for the bright lights of the city.

One of the principal aspects of the Turner Hypothesis is the idea that the wilderness of the West had defined the American character, breeding the virtues of democracy, individualism and egalitarianism and

117 Frederick Jackson Turner, "The Significance of the Frontier," in *The Early Writings of Frederick Jackson Turner* (Madison, WI: State Historical Society of Wisconsin, 1938), 14.

118 Ibid., 186.

119 Ibid.

120 Smith, *Virgin Land*, 206.

121 Ibid.

providing a purifying influence in contrast to the materialism and vice that characterized city life.[122] The new wording in this stanza invests the "range" with a heavy symbolic value, distinguishing rural from urban and east from west while extolling the virtues of nature during a period of increasing growth of urban centres.

During the Progressive Era in America, popular films often portrayed the hardworking cowboy as the hero, in contrast to the eastern "city slicker," who represented "the corrupting influence of the city."[123] However, the cowboy had not always been treated so kindly. At the time when "Home on the Range" became a song, cowboys were not the romantic heroes they later became. In the 1870s, when the poem/song was written, "cowboy" was used predominantly as a pejorative term that "usually called up the image of a semibarbarous laborer who lived a dull, monotonous life of hard fare and poor shelter."[124] However, in 1885, the year that "Colorado Home" was written, there was already a sense among Americans that "the wild and wonderful western frontier was rapidly disappearing, and that the winning of the West must be lived vicariously through the heroes who tamed it."[125] After the gold rushes of the late nineteenth century,[126] the mantle passed from the farmer and miner to the American cowboy—and "Home on the Range" followed suit.

As every child who has played cowboys and Indians knows, the cowboy's natural enemy is the Native North American, and the fourth verse of the McCurry/Lomax version of the song serves as a poignant reminder of the outcome of that conflict. By the time the song was written, European Americans and Native Americans had been engaged in full-scale hostilities on the western frontier for a decade,[127] and it is not characteristic of the cowboy as typically portrayed to have conflicted feelings about the genocide of Native Americans. However, when

122 Edward N. Saveth, ed., *Understanding the American Past: American History and Its Interpretation*, 2nd ed. (Boston: Little, Brown, 1965), 15.

123 Green, *Singing in the Saddle*, 31.

124 Smith, *Virgin Land*, 99.

125 Green, *Singing in the Saddle*, 6.

126 Biemiller, "The Land Sings Its History," 79.

127 West, *Way to the West*, 48.

speculating on the significance of this verse to the cowboys, it is important to remember that the song as recorded by Lomax would have been only one of many versions circulating, and no doubt there were numerous other verses that were left out by McCurry. Mechem posits: "it is likely that this [verse] was a stray or a maverick, favored by the Negro singer who had picked it up on the Chisholm Trail."[128]

Regardless of its general acceptance at the time, the very existence of the verse marks an important moment in the history of a song that had previously omitted any sense of the price paid for the establishment of these successive "Western Homes." As historian David W. Noble writes, settlers like Higley repressed the implications of their presence for the Native Americans by casting Native Americans as "underdeveloped, not fully human, and incapable of living in freedom"—they were seen as a "people without history."[129] Thus white settlers could solve the dilemma of why the land that made them free did not do the same for its original inhabitants.[130]

The added verse about the "red man" in the Lomax/McCurry version of "Home on the Range" simply introduces this effect of western settlement without commenting on it. Presumably written sometime between 1873 and 1908, the intentions behind the verse can only be speculated on, but its inclusion offers the first evidence in the song of an awareness of the price paid by some so that others could enjoy their "Home on the Range."

128 Mechem, *Story of Home on the Range*, 24.

129 David W. Noble, *Death of a Nation: American Culture and the End of Exceptionalism* (Minneapolis: University of Minnesota Press, 2002), xiii.

130 George Lipitz, foreword to Noble, *Death of a Nation*, xiii.

131 Lomax, *Adventures*, xii.

OH, GIVE ME A HOME

After "Home on the Range" was published in Lomax's *Cowboy Songs and Other Frontier Ballads*, the printed version went almost unnoticed for fifteen years.[131] Then, in 1925, Carl Fischer produced the first sheet music, and in 1930, David Guion wrote another arrangement, which in the ensuing eight years was followed by an increasing number of slight variations as the song's popularity continued to grow.[132] The Guion version was sung on the radio and incorporated into the concert programs of singers Lawrence Tibbett and John Charles Thomas, further raising the song's profile.[133]

This transition from the oral to popular print tradition marked another significant turning point for "Home on the Range," and the growing demand for the sheet music had its own implications for the song. However, according to Mechem, it wasn't until 1933, when president-elect Franklin D. Roosevelt endorsed it as his favourite song, that "Home on the Range" became the most popular tune in America.[134] As Mechem writes, in the period immediately following Roosevelt's statement, "such sudden and worldwide success was probably never equaled by another song."[135]

Hickman attributes the success of the song to much more than the president-elect's approval. The year that marks the beginning of the song's astronomical rise in popularity was also the year the Great Depression reached its lowest depths. As Hickman argues, "[T]he refrain that helped to dispel the gloom of the 'Grasshopper Days' in Kansas, and had brought renewed hope to the hard pressed pioneer throughout the West, was a most appropriate song for the Great Depression and the era of the New Deal."[136] The optimism that had so appealed to pioneers in hard times resonated with Americans in the grips of a worldwide economic crisis. And beyond merely creating a desire for cheerful songs in general, the Great Depression provided fertile ground for the success of this particular song, because it was the favourite of a figure who became immensely popular during that period: the singing cowboy.

Peter Stanfield, author of *Horse Opera: The Strange History of the 1930s Singing Cowboy*, calls this character "one of the most important cultural figures to emerge from the tumultuous years of

132 Croy, *Corn Country*, 171.

133 Lomax, *Adventures*, 61–64.

134 Mechem, *Story of Home on the Range*, 2.

135 Ibid.

136 Hickman, "Historical Background," 23.

the Great Depression."[137] This was a character, writes Stanfield, who "represented the fantasies, desires, and ambitions of those who felt keenly the economic hardship and the threat (and fact) of dispossession and dislocation."[138] As Gene Autry wrote in his preface to the ballad book, *He Was Singin' This Song*, "The romanticized life of the cowboy—his valor and fortitude in the face of every kind of · hardship—was admired by Americans whose own courage was being tested by the depression."[139] And this fascination was not unique to the cowboy's home range. "A lot of folks had the idea my records were only popular in the Midwest," writes Autry, "but I actually sold more recordings in eastern states and New England."[140] As a result of the singing cowboy's appeal, cowboy and western songs enjoyed unprecedented popularity in the early 1930s, and "Home on the Range" was the most popular among them.[141]

The emergence of the singing cowboy coincided with the decline of genuine cowboy culture and caused the cowboy's complex history to be obscured through commercial exploitation of his image.[142] The economic crisis had shattered the myth of the garden, thereby marking what Henry Nash Smith calls the "real end of the frontier period."[143] In an attempt to hold onto this dream, Americans latched onto the last denizen of this disappearing world.[144] As a result, the fictional cowboy eclipsed the real cowboy, and it was through this fabricated figure that Americans continued to imagine the West well into the 20th century.

Western-themed Broadway musicals portrayed camp renditions of the cowboy lifestyle, and Western movies enthralled urban audiences with their unrealistic depictions of life on the frontier.[145] "The East has met the West in cowboy song literature," wrote John Lomax in 1938, "and has sucked up its treasures."[146] This fabrication had a price. As Stanfield

137 Peter Stanfield, *Horse Opera: The Strange History of the 1930s Singing Cowboy* (Chicago: University of Illinois Press, 2002), 3.

138 Ibid.

139 Gene Autry, preface to Tinsley, *He Was Singin' This Song*, ix.

140 Ibid.

141 Tinsley, *He Was Singin' This Song*, 215.

142 Stanfield, *Horse Opera*, 1.

143 Smith, *Virgin Land*, 188.

144 Lomax, *Cowboy Songs*, xxvii.

145 Ibid., xx.

146 Ibid.

argues, "[T]he view of the singing cowboy as little more than a Saturday matinee distraction for kids, a nostalgic figure for more innocent times, or, more recently, a prime example of American camp has effaced his real history."[147] The same can be said of "Home on the Range" itself. The commercial appropriation of the song, which exploited its wealth of accumulated cultural currency, diluted its original power as much as it broadened the range of its popularity.

Meanwhile, the natural landscape that Higley lauded in his poem was vanishing. The curlew and swan had long since disappeared from Smith County.[148] The buffalo was virtually extinct.[149] And the "glittering stream" had dried up, clogged with silt as a result of erosion of prairie grasses by wagon wheels and overgrazing cattle and other domestic animals.[150] These developments were not new— immigrants had been burning, felling, digging and hunting their way through the country's natural resources for generations—but by the 1930s, the effects of this overuse were undeniable. In 1938 John Lomax wrote,

> Gone are the buffalo, the Indian warwhoop, the free grass of the open plain—even the stinging lizard, the tarantula, the horned frog, the centipede, the prairie dog, the rattle-snake, the Gila monster, the vinegarroon, are fast disappearing. Save in some of the secluded valleys of southern New Mexico, the old-time round-up is no more; the trails to Kansas and to Montana have become grass-grown or lost in fields of waving grain.[151]

By the 1930s the Turner Hypothesis provided the dominant view of American history.[152] And while dissenting voices called for a move toward agrarian simplicity and away from materialism

147 Stanfield, *Horse Opera*, 1.

148 Mechem, *Story of Home on the Range*, 23.

149 Ibid., 18.

150 Croy, *Corn Country*, 168; West, *Way to the West*, 31.

151 Lomax, *Cowboy Songs*, xxvii.

152 Kerwin Klein, *Frontiers of Historical Imagination: Narrating the European Conquest of Native America* (Berkeley: University of California Press, 1997), 8.

and industrialization,[153] the majority still viewed the land as something to be conquered and exploited as the American people pursued their manifest destiny. As journalist Adams wrote of his impressions during his 1939 drive west across the United States, "[T]he pioneer tradition and the will to conquer and subdue the land, no matter what difficulties it presents, are not yet dead in this country."[154] The evidence of this is the existence of "thousands upon thousands of well-kept homes," which Adams passes as he drives across the country, "homes of the great mass of self-respecting, hard-working American citizens. There is nothing like it on a similar scale anywhere else in the world."[155] Thus, in Adams's view at least, rather than the beauty of nature, it is the home itself, the physical brick and mortar house, that has become the symbol of the promise of America and proof of the realization of the American dream.

THE WESTERN HOME

153 Klein, *Frontiers of Historical Imagination*, 8; Kolodny, *Lay of the Land*, 139.

154 Adams, "A New Yorker," 21.

155 Ibid., 10.

156 H. Craig Miner, *The History of the Sunflower State, 1854-2000* (Lawrence: University Press of Kansas, 2002), 318.

157 Robert W. Richmond and Robert W. Mardock, *A Nation Moving West: Readings in the History of the American Frontier* (Lincoln: University of Nebraska Press, 1966), 282.

In 1947, "Home on the Range" became the official state song of Kansas. However, the official version, while keeping the title probably given by the cowboys, reverted in most other respects to the original poem that appeared in the *Smith County Pioneer* in 1873. By that time there were no buffalo roaming in the area, but one member of the legislature joked: "knocking out buffalo and putting in Jersey milk cow would naturally hob with the meter of the thing."[156] The presumably unintended aptness of this statement might have been lost in a period when Kansan legislators sought to encourage the expansion of agricultural productivity, which had reached unprecedented levels during the Second World War.[157]

Some Kansans were not pleased with the choice of "Home on the Range" as their state song. "Some say it is too mournful," writes Mechem, "and others complain that it fails to 'sell' the state and its products."[158] During this period of postwar economic prosperity and the growth of big business,[159] "Home on the Range" again became a vehicle for the preoccupations of the time. On June 18, 1948, the Kansas Industrial Development Commission announced in *The Western Star* a one hundred dollar contest to "find a parody to the official state song": "The new stanzas should paint a word picture of Kansas—its bountiful agriculture, diversified industry, vast and varied natural resources, scenic beauty, the fine people of our state and various sections of the state such as the rich Flint Hills area."[160]

These new verses were intended for use in commercials that would advertise the state's agriculture and industry. They were also used for political purposes, and were first introduced at the inauguration celebration for Governor Frank Carlson in January 1949.[161] On this occasion, writes Mechem, "the music was jazzed to such a pitch that if the tune had been so played when first written all the deer and antelope would have been scared out of the country."[162]

There was some backlash against the use of the song for commercial purposes, and many wrote to legislators and published letters in the newspaper protesting this appropriation of the state song. "Although this protest may have been only a natural reaction against singing commercials," writes Mechem, "it is more likely that the song expresses emotions that go deeper than a desire for bigger business."[163] However, despite these dissenting voices, the Kansan authorities continued their attempts to shine up the image of the famous song to maximize its utility as a draw to the state.

In 1946, Homer Croy visited the site of Higley's claim in Smith County, Kansas. The dugout in which Higley had been living when he wrote "Home on the Range" was gone, replaced by a log cabin, built

158 Mechem, *Story of Home on the Range*, 25.

159 Noble, *Death of a Nation*, 349.

160 "Find a parody," *The Western Star*, 12.

161 Mechem, *Story of Home on the Range*, 25.

162 Ibid.

163 Ibid., 26.

179

in 1875, in which Higley lived with his fifth wife, Sarah E. Clemans.[164] This log cabin is often still incorrectly referred to as the place where "Home on the Range" was written.[165] At the time of Croy's visit in 1946, the cabin and surrounding property were owned by a man named Pete Rust, who was accustomed to receiving visitors to the site. But as Croy approached what was to him a place of pilgrimage, he was shocked by what he saw:

> By now we arrived at the cabin. I nearly fell over. It is now a henhouse! It's filled with white hens with red combs, and smells to the top of the trees ... I hadn't yet got over my shock. "Couldn't you clean out the old cabin and keep it for sentimental reasons?" Pete Rust shook his head. "We're short of hen space." "Don't you ever pause and look at it and think what a historical event took place here?" "Yes, I do sometimes," said Pete reflectively. "On the other hand, I've got used to the idea. An' there's always the hen-space problem. I have to think of that."[166]

In Croy's view, this was one more example of the indignities that the song increasingly had to endure in a rapidly changing world. Croy notes that the Smith Center Chamber of Commerce had purchased land to create a park in the town of Smith Center and planned to relocate Higley's cabin there. The move, the authorities reasoned, would make the cabin more easily accessible to tourists, since the original location was too far from the highway.[167]

"I would rather think of it being on the banks of the Beaver," writes Croy, "even if the cabin is filled with chickens—than I would in a tourist-catching park."[168] But if the goal was to preserve the place where the famous song originated, then it did not matter where the cabin was, because it was not the "home on the range." The real home in need of preservation was the open space, clean air, fresh water and abundant

164 Hickman, "Historical Background," 17.

165 Mechem, *Story of Home on the Range*, 14.

166 Croy, *Corn Country*, 168.

167 Ibid., 179.

168 Ibid.

wildlife that had been in decline due to human activities since before Higley wrote the poem.

This anecdote exemplifies the pastoral paradox: human beings seeking communion with nature set out into the wilderness, but their very presence erodes the wilderness that they seek. What Howard Mumford Jones calls "the emotional appeal of the uncharted forest, the unfenced range, the trackless mountains and the open sky"— the world that Higley described—was the very attraction that led to the destruction of that world.[169] As Annette Kolodny writes, "[T]he success of settlement depended on the ability to master the land, transforming the virgin territories into something else—a farm, a village, a road, a canal, a railway, a mine, a factory, a city, and finally, an urban nation."[170] But like many dreams, the dream of the "garden of the West" outlived the hope of its realization, and nostalgia for a simpler time led to displaced significance being attributed to Higley's cabin, which was itself almost displaced from the landscape that was its reason for being.

However, by making Higley's cabin the shrine to "Home on the Range," the Kansan authorities provided a fitting conclusion to that chapter of the song's story. From the beginning, "Home on the Range" was a story about an imagined place that became a blank canvas onto which the pastoral longings of successive generations could be projected. From the garden of the West to the riches of the mine to a nostalgic rendering of a lost idyll, the song has always represented an impulse that has shaped and motivated the American cultural dream life since the docking of the Mayflower: the quest for a home.

169 Kolodny, *Lay of the Land*, 18.

170 Ibid., 7.

A version of this article first appeared as Cooper, C.M. 2011. From "No Place" to Home: The Quest for a Western Home in Brewster Higley's "Home on the Range." *Great Plains Quarterly*, Vol. 31, No. 4, pp. 267-90.

The Western Home is a work of fiction. The story of the song is told through the stories of the people who helped shape its destiny by writing, rewriting, singing, recording, claiming and disowning it. Just as these people adapted the song to reflect what was important to them, I have adapted their personal histories to tell the story of the song. This telling reflects my own projections and fantasies about the West and about the past—I believe that this is both fitting and, to a certain extent at least, inevitable. I have used archival documents and historical personages and places, but I have invented characters, scenes and dialogue and altered facts to fit the needs of the work. In several of the stories I have included incidents and quotations attributed to or recorded by the historical characters depicted, both in official and personal correspondence and in (auto)biographical works. Significantly, "Here in the Grass We Will Lie" is a retelling of Homer Croy's visit with Brewster Higley's son and his family, which Croy recorded in the book *Corn Country*; "Seeing the Elephant" is loosely based on events described by John Lomax in his autobiography, *Adventures of a Ballad Hunter*; "The Solomon Vale" is based on a true crime that happened in Eastern Canada in the nineteenth century; and "Report of Samuel Moanfeldt, on his Investigation" is a fictional retelling of Moanfeldt's 1935 report of the same name. Some details in this story and in "Medicine Song" were inspired by the travel writing of Ernie Pyle.

THANKS TO my teacher, Terence Byrnes. To Peter Heron for his help, advice and encouragement. To my dear friends Mary Katherine Carr, Sarah Faber, Susan Paddon, Jocelyn Parr and Rebecca Silver Slayter. To Arts Nova Scotia, for financially supporting my work through the Grants to Individuals Program, which allowed me the privilege of focusing on my writing full-time. To El Dean Holthus and the rest of the Home on the Range Trustees. To Norman and Dianne McNeill. To Nicola Nixon and Kate Sterns. To Francesco de Cardona for giving me a beautiful place to live in Rome while I revised this manuscript. To Tracy Monaghan. To Jonáš Koukl. To Cathey Heron for her help researching "Medicine Song." To Jim French for his help researching "The Solomon Vale." To my father, Phillip Cooper, for his help with the medical details in "The Western Home." To Matthew Parsons for his editorial advice on my *Great Plains Quarterly* essay. To Emily Parker for her help researching "Nuclear Heartland." To Michael Redhill, Nadia Szilvassy and everyone else at *Brick*, whose publication of "Nuclear Heartland" led to the publication of this book. To Beth Follett for her kindness as a person and careful attention as an editor. To my mother, Eleanor Harper, for everything. To Ivor Harper, who I never knew, but whose presence I have often felt.

The first full version of "Home on the Range" that I ever read was in a book called *Good Poems*, edited by Garrison Keillor. Although

I only knew the chorus, as I think most North Americans do, I felt a special connection to the song because my mother had always told me that it was the favourite song of her father, Ivor, who died when she was twelve. This version, which is credited as "Anonymous," and which is very different from the original version, was what made me want to write this book. I'd like to thank whoever wrote it.*

Home on the Range

There's a land in the West where nature is blessed
With a beauty so vast and austere,
And though you have flown off to cities unknown,
Your memories bring you back here.

Home, home on the range
Where the deer and the antelope play,
Where seldom is heard a discouraging word
And the skies are not cloudy all day.

Where the air is so pure, the zephyrs so free,
The breezes so balmy and light,
That I would not exchange my home on the range
For all of the cities so bright.

How often at night when the heavens are bright
With the light of the glittering stars,
Have I stood here amazed and asked as I gazed
If their glory exceeds that of ours.

Where the teepees were raised in a cool shady place
By the rivers where sweet grasses grew

Where the bison was found on the great hunting ground
And fed all the nations of Sioux

The canyons and buttes, like old twisted roots
And the sandstone of ancient stream beds,
In the sunset they rise to dazzle our eyes
With their lavenders, yellows and reds.

Oh, give me a land where the bright diamond sand
Flows leisurely down to the stream,
Where the graceful white swan goes gliding along
Like a maid in a heavenly dream.

When it comes to my time to leave this world behind
And fly off to regions unknown,
Please lay my remains out here on the plains,
At rest in my sweet prairie home.

Home, home on the plains
Here in the grass we will lie
When our day's work is done by the light of the sun
And it sets in the blue prairie sky.

* I have made every effort to confirm
  permissions, though unsuccessfully.

The Hut

Up the hill is a hut made of sound
where two windows rhyme
and the tiles stay on
because they are nailed to a dream.
The dreamer wonders: Can this be mine?

The floor is solid and straight
and is amber from sap.
The walls don't leak or let out heat
from gray embers in the grate.

This is the original home
at the heart of brutalist design.
No storm can slam its shape apart.
No thief can carry it off like a tent.
It dwells in ashen buildings where the present sleeps.

*

"This poem is a new and unpublished poem of mine that expresses my wish for every poem and at the same time attempts to reflect that wish in the structure of this poem. It is very simple and shows the narrator, the first person, as someone without attributes, a dream-self really, who can still imagine, and even see, the original form that underlies all other forms, no matter how "brutalist" in design they have become. This structure can't be destroyed or blown away or robbed. It belongs to the world of the unconscious, which is the source of all that is solid and sensory. It is air-tight, and still warm, but buried under historical forces."

— FANNY HOWE

Fanny Howe has written more than twenty books, including novels, essays and, of course, poetry. She currently makes her home in Martha's Vineyard.

CATHERINE COOPER'S fiction was published most recently in *Brick* magazine, her non-fiction in *Guernica* magazine. Her first novel, *White Elephant*, is forthcoming. She lives in Prague, Czech Republic. *The Western Home* is her first book.